Barry Crump wrote his fir[...] Man, in 1960. It became [...] numerous other books wh[...] famous and best-loved New Zealand character is [...] Cash, who features in *Hang on a Minute Mate*, Crump's second book. Between them, these two books have sold over 400,000 copies and continue to sell at an amazing rate some 30 years later.

Crump began his working life as a professional hunter, culling deer and pigs in some of the ruggedest country in New Zealand. After the runaway success of his first book, he pursued many diverse activities, including goldmining, radio talkback, white-baiting, television presenting, crocodile shooting and acting.

As to classifying his occupation, Crump always insisted that he was a Kiwi bushman.

He published 25 books and was awarded the MBE for services to literature in 1994.

SHORTY

Books by Barry Crump

A Good Keen Man (1960)
Hang on a Minute Mate (1961)
One of Us (1962)
There and Back (1963)
Gulf (1964) – now titled *Crocodile Country*
Scrapwaggon (1965)
The Odd Spot of Bother (1967)
No Reference Intended (1968)
Warm Beer and Other Stories (1969)
A Good Keen Girl (1970)
Bastards I Have Met (1970)
Fred (1972)
Shorty (1980)
Puha Road (1982)
The Adventures of Sam Cash (1985)
Wild Pork and Watercress (1986)
Barry Crump's Bedtime Yarns (1988)
Bullock Creek (1989)
The Life and Times of a Good Keen Man (1992)
Gold and Greenstone (1993)
Arty and the Fox (1994)
Forty Yarns and a Song (1995)
Mrs Windyflax and the Pungapeople (1995)
Crumpy's Campfire Companion (1996)
As the Saying Goes (1996)
A Tribute to Crumpy: Barry Crump 1935–1996 is an anthology of tributes, extracts from Crump's books, letters and pictures from his private photo collection.

All titles currently (1997) in print.

SHORTY

BARRY CRUMP WROTE IT

Rick Welland decorated it

Hodder Moa Beckett

First published in 1980 by CW Associates

This edition published in 1997

ISBN 1-86958-547-X

© 1980 Barry Crump

Published by Hodder Moa Beckett Publishers Limited
[a member of the Hodder Headline Group]
4 Whetu Place, Mairangi Bay, Auckland, New Zealand

Typeset by TTS Jazz, Auckland

Cover photo: Photobank

Printed by Wright and Carman (NZ) Ltd, New Zealand

No reference intended to anyone in this book.
It's a slice of lunacy.

CONTENTS

PRIL

Arney knows how I feel about having introductions forced on me, and he only ever brings people over to my place if he thinks I'll get on okay with them. (Arney Sutton's my neighbour, by the way. Good bloke too. One of the best). So when he brought this other bloke over to meet me a couple of weeks back I knew he reckoned it was the right thing to do. He's not always right, Arney, but he always means well, and that's worth a lot of points as far as I'm concerned.

The bloke he had with him this time was called Jerry Marshall. They'd run across each other in the pub and got to talking about pig-hunting, and one thing led to another and in the end Arney brought Jerry out to meet me because I've got the best pig-dogs around here — three of them at the moment — and this Jerry was dead keen to have a go at it.

Well, nearly all the cows were dried off for the winter and there was a bit of spare time around. The dogs needed a run too, and this Jerry bloke seemed like a decent-enough sort, when you got to know him a bit. We arranged for me to take him out on Thursday afternoon — no guarantee we were going to get anything, and I carry the only rifle we take with us. He was right on for it.

It turned out that Jerry was a professional golfer. He worked over at the Mt. Garlon golf course, so I picked him up there and we went to a place I know up in the Kaimais and put the dogs through a few gullies.

By four o'clock that afternoon we were back at the ute with a nice young eating-pig each, all singed-up and ready for the pot. Jerry was tickled pink about it, and when I dropped him off at his place he offered to give me a few free golf lessons if I was interested.

The closest I'd ever been to a golf course, as far as I could remember, was when I'd picked him up earlier that day. He reckoned that it was easier to teach someone who'd never done it before because there were no bad habits to correct. I thought it over for a bit and decided to take him up on his offer.

By the way, my name's Lance Butler, but my *real close* friends sometimes call be Shorty. I'm five foot-four, if you must know. Not that my height's got anything to do with it. Don't know how it cropped up at all, come to think of it. Sorry about that, just forget it, will you. Pleased to meet you, whoever you are.

Anyway, I met Jerry out at the Mt. Garlon Golf Club a couple of days later ready for my golf instruction. Not too many people about. I was expecting to get stuck into a game right off, and sort of pick up the rules and things as I went along, but there's a bit more to this golfing caper than you'd think.

The first thing you find out is that there's different sorts of clubs for different sorts of shots, and there's a special tricky way of hanging onto them. You can't just chuck a ball on the ground and clout it one — I tried that.

For openers you're supposed to sit the ball up on a little plastic peg that looks like a cross between a Y and a wedge, but they call it a Tee. Then there's a special way you have to stand to swing the waddy. It's not too easy to get the hang of, either. You can dig up a fair bit of turf trying to get it right.

After about an hour of practising swinging the club around, Jerry let me have a go at actually hitting a golf ball. It's tricky, all right! After a bit of that he reckoned I was getting remarkably good at it. He hadn't expected me to pick it up so quick and decided to take me round a few holes to get the feel of the game.

I hit off first, right down one side of this long narrow paddock and into the trees on the opposite side. Don't ask me how it went like that, but it did! It wasn't *too* bad, Jerry reckoned, because I could still get another crack at it, which seems to be fairly important. Apparently you're supposed to stick with the same ball right up till you lose it.

A lot of these things are hard for us slightly-shorter blokes. For instance the handles of all those golf sticks were far too long for me. I had to stand a lot further away from the ball than Jerry. Anyway it took me eight goes with different clubs to get my second ball up to where his first shot landed. He made it look real easy.

I had to hand it to Jerry, he was pretty patient with me, especially seeing as he was so good at it and me being a mug at the game. I suppose he was used to teaching beginners.

On about my twelfth shot — Jerry was keeping track of how many shots and balls we were using, it's part of the rules — anyway, on about my twelfth shot the ball bounced over a bit of a rise and landed fair in one of those eroded patches you quite often see around golf courses — Looked like a bit of good luck to me at first, because it saved the thing going any further in the wrong direction. But it turned out that it would have been better to have actually missed it altogether. It was just like Jerry said: a proper bloody sand-trap!

It took me seven goes to get the ball out of there. Must have been getting a bit hacked off with it by the time I finally clouted it right, because it went quite a bit too far. About a hundred yards, actually. And four clouts later it was back in the same hole again. I wasn't going through all that again, so I picked it up and threw it out of there. Didn't want Jerry to get sick of waiting around for me.

They ought to do something about getting some of those blasted things filled in. They must ruin more games of golf than you could poke a stick at. A couple of blokes with shovels could level one of them off in an hour or two. No idea, some people! And you'd think with all the time and money they put into the game they could afford to get some of those trees knocked down. Then they'd be able to burn off a few of the scrubby patches and bring the whole place into grass.

It'd sure make it a lot easier for them. Funny, though, Jerry didn't seem at all taken with the idea when I suggested it. I was only trying to help.

Maybe I'd better explain a bit about the actual game of golf, in case you haven't had a go at it yourself yet. First off, any number of people can play at once, but they usually keep it down to about four — probably to save confusion. I found out that they can get quite snarky if you get your ball mixed up with theirs. Another thing is that the men and women play on different days. This has probably got something to do with the language they use sometimes. Quite an eye-opener, that, and men and women never like each other to hear them swearing.

They don't like lending anyone their clubs and everybody wheels a whole bunch of them around on a trolley kind of gadget. (Jerry did actually tell me what the right name of those trolleys is, but I've forgotten). Anyway the whole idea of the game is to see who can hit a golf ball right round the course, using the least number of hits and balls. You can use as many clubs as you like, by the look of it. It pays to keep the ball you're hitting away from the trees and long grass, and especially any water that's around, but that's not easy. Some of those pools must be half full of golf balls! You're not supposed to pick the ball up and throw it out into the open, or even give it a kick, once the game's started. It's just not done, Jerry reckons.

Then there's the flags. You've probably seen them sticking up every here and there on golf courses. There's a special reason for those flags. If you take a closer look you'll see that there's a patch of real short grass around each flagpole. Looks as if it's been overstocked with sheep, but in fact they use mowers on it. And each flagpole is sitting in the middle of a large baked-bean tin set into the ground.

The idea is that you're not supposed to go past any of the flags without potting your ball in the hole the flag's in. There's a special club for that, too. After you've done that you pick up your ball and go over to the place for what they call teeing-off towards the next flag. Quite simple, really, once you get the idea of it.

You might find some of the rules a bit hard to handle at first. For instance, if your ball gets lost, or *has* to be picked up and carted out to where you can get a decent swipe at it, they add a couple of shots onto your score. As though you're not in enough strife already! It's probably to make you more careful next time, or something like that.

Another thing I picked up pretty early on is that even the experts can come undone at golf! And if *they* can, you needn't feel too bad about your own miscalculations.

Jerry was more than a hundred hits ahead of me at the twelfth flag. And when he teed off for the thirteenth flag he blew the shot something terrible! Right off the golf course and across the other side of the road. He didn't even bother to go and have a look for it. He probably gets plenty of balls cheap anyway, being a pro and all that.

Then he did another funny thing. He rammed the club back into the bag so hard the stitching came away round the bottom and for the rest of the game he had to tow his trolley along with all these handles dragging on the grass.

He took eleven hits to get his ball into the hole that time, and I only took nineteen, so I figured he must have been getting worried in case I caught him up. Couldn't see how, though, but in case it made him feel better I let him know I was trying to let him get ahead a bit more.

But it's a funny game, golf. The less you try the better you seem to get. Between the sixteenth and seventeenth flags I only used eight hits. Jerry used seven and tried to kid me he usually did it in four. I found that one a bit hard to swallow, but he was obviously worried about something or other so I let it pass.

What with all the obstacles and a bit of hard luck here and there, plus the fact of me being a bit green at the game, it took me a hundred and sixty-eight hits to get right round the eighteen or nineteen different flags. Must have been a bad day for playing golf because Jerry took eighty-nine hits himself and he'd told me before he started that the most he'd ever taken to get round that particular course was seventy-eight with the course half under water.

After you've got right round the course you go to the clubhouse. Bar and all, just like a pub only quieter. Less people too. It must be a hell of a strain on those professional golfers, teaching people how to do it. Jerry had to sink four double whiskies before he could even talk to his mates!

I ended up yarning with some of the other golf players in there. Members of the club, they were. Not a bad bunch of blokes, once you got talking to them, and from what they told me there's even more to know about playing golf.

For one thing, you're always supposed to wear those spiked shoes to play in. Actually they don't usually let you on the course — or even in the clubhouse, wearing gumboots. Talk about embarrassing! It was only because I was a personal guest of the club pro that no one had said anything about it. Another thing you're not allowed to do is miss out any of the flags. Even if you do accidently find yourself handier to another one, you're supposed to go right back to the one you aimed at first, even if it puts you up over the two hundred mark! Something to do with the flow of golfers around the course, I gathered.

Something else I found out was that the hunks of turf you rip out of the ground when you hit the ball a bit low are called "divots", but seeing as I hadn't taken anything I didn't think it could have possibly applied to me!

I offered to nick round and patch up the holes I'd dug, but they were pretty decent about it and told me not to bother.

There's even more to it than that. A lot of stuff about cards and handicaps, but it was all way over my head.

In spite of the rules being against you, and all the trees and humps and hollows and sand-traps and stuff, I enjoyed that game of golf. In fact I wouldn't mind having another go at it some time. I reckon I could get round one of those golf courses with less than a hundred shots if I put my mind to it.

I've been trying to get in touch with Jerry to see if I can jack up another game, but he's been a bit hard to contact just lately.

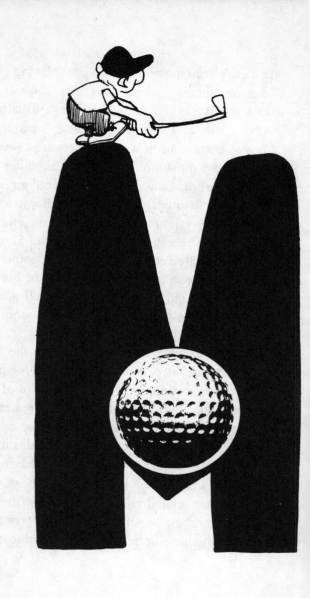

AY

Forget everything I said about golf before. I've had a bit of experience since then and found out a whole lot more about the game. For instance, I didn't realize at first that they deliberately make it tough so you have to develop your cunning to be able to compete! But anyway, here's what happened.

After that first somewhat embarrassing game with my golf pro mate Jerry Marshall, I might never have got back into golf again, except that we found this old set of clubs in Arney's implement-shed when we were looking for a bundle of possum traps he thought he had in there. Well it wasn't exactly a set; there were four of them. A number-three wood (even had a wooden handle!), a number-six iron in quite good nick except that some of the chrome was peeling off the handle and the grip needed building up with insulation tape, a number-two iron with a slight bend in the handle, and a putter that everyone we've showed it to reckons is a fair-dinkum antique!

Not exactly what you'd call a matched set, but plenty good enough to start off with. And they were housed in one of those First-World-War leather rifle-scabbards. All I had to do was rig a bit of rope on it to carry it with and I was in business!

Then I had another stroke of luck; I caught Jerry on the phone out at the golf club and put it on him for another game. He didn't seem all that terribly enthusiastic at first, but when I told him I'd actually got myself a set of clubs he settled down a bit and said that if I got myself some proper golf shoes and promised to practise hitting the balls the way he'd showed me, he'd try and fit me in the following Friday if he wasn't too tied up. Real decent of him, I thought, considering how busy he is these days!

Then I had a real good idea, I made a deal with Arney's two eldest boys to supply me with up to a dozen golf balls. Twenty cents each. They've been trying to get enough money together to buy a pushbike each. They don't know it, but Arney and I are going to shout them the balance once they've earned half the money for themselves.

While they were hunting up the balls I practised my swing by grubbing out practically all the thistles in the road paddock with my six-iron. I can recommend this idea. You shouldn't have any trouble getting permission from any farmer with a paddock full of thistles. Doesn't work too good with ragwort or gorse plants, though.

Arney's boys came back with twenty-six golf balls! Far too many, as I thought at the time, and I only bought a dozen of them at first. Some of them were a bit rumpty, anyway.

Then I suffered a minor setback. There's a bigger difference between thistles and golf balls than I'd allowed for. The thistles seemed to go straight enough, but when I applied my newly acquired skill to a golf ball it was everything but straight. There was something wrong. I got Arney's missus to pick me up a book about golf for beginners when she went into town.

That night I settled down to swot up on it. And it wasn't too long before I'd figured out what I was doing wrong. With thoughts of how knocked out Jerry was going to be when I gave him a close go in our next game, I couldn't wait to try it out.

It was dark by this time, so I set up a ball in the light from the back porch and clouted it fair out into the paddock somewhere. It felt pretty good, so I tried it again, but this time I heard the ball hit the roof of the cowshed. Away out to the left — but now I had the book. I could figure out what I was doing wrong.

Within half an hour I was getting it right! I hopped into the ute and shot over to Arney's place and got his missus to wake up the boys and bought the rest of their golf balls off them. By about midnight I was out of balls again, but I could tell I was really getting somewhere, especially with the six-iron.

After milking next morning I scouted around the paddock and found nine golf balls. I spent most of the day practising and by milking time that afternoon I only had three balls left. (There's a big raupo swamp alongside our road paddock). But I was really getting into the swing of it. I could tell! All I needed was the golf shoes and I was ready for the big match with Jerry!

To cut a long story short I scored a second-hand pair of golf shoes for six bucks at the auction mart in town. Must have been ladies' shoes because they were a bit small for me. I split them up the back and laced a bit of electrical-wire across. Worked okay. Arney reckoned I was going a bit overboard on the game, but he was only hacked off because I wouldn't go pig-hunting with him, and I've got the best pig-dogs around here.

Found five more golf balls around the paddock next day during practice and still had four of them left when I fronted up at the golf club on the Friday morning to challenge Jerry to the big one! He didn't have a great deal to say about my clubs when I showed them to him, but that wasn't going to worry me. What did worry me for a while was that I'd completely overlooked getting a supply of those little perches for the balls they call tees. But — and here's a good tip — you can find plenty of them if you just scout around the hitting-off places. I picked up six of them right outside the clubhouse! Then I had to scout around and find Jerry again. But finally we were ready to tee off again.

He gave me fifty shots' start and the deal was that if I won he'd have another game with me next week, and if he won I had to find someone else to play with and pay what they call "green fees". I was pretty confident of giving him a good run for his money this time, but I didn't say anything, which turned out to be just as well.

I hit off first, and when I say off, I mean way off. Right off! Somehow I hit the ground before the ball and didn't even see where it went. Jerry had to tell me; round the corner of the clubhouse. But I was only learning still. I suggested that we wipe that shot and start afresh and he immediately refused, quite unreasonably, I thought. Not done, he reckoned. And he wasn't any happier with his first shot than I'd been with mine. I'd have been pleased enough to have been able to hit one like he did, though.

I decided to leave the wood-club in the bag for the time being and tee off with my two-iron. When Jerry saw the bend in the handle he wanted to call the game off, but I hit the ball nearly as far as his had gone. He *had* to carry on. After that I was into my favourite six-iron and really showed him a trick. My second shot landed right beside the green and his was sixty yards short. Six putts wasn't too bad, considering I'd never had any practice. We ended up with him taking four shots for the first hole and me taking ten.

He was inclined to be a bit scathing about my putter, but later on in the game I offered to lend it to him because his one didn't seem to be working properly.

As we were belting them up the fairway (that's the main run-way for golf balls) towards the third hole, it started raining. And by the time we were ready to tee off for the fourth hole Jerry wanted to turn it in and head back to the clubhouse. But I'd been swotting up on the rules and you're not allowed to terminate a game of golf because of the weather. Jerry should have known about that, being a pro. He was lucky I pointed it out to him, actually. He could have lost the game by default!

We played on. And then I caught him out on another one. He'd given up writing down his score, but I was keeping a note of it and made him bring his scoring-card up to scratch. No doubt about these pros, is there! They're up to all the tricks.

By the time we'd done nine holes I'd used up my fifty-shot handicap, but there were only eleven shots between our scores. Jerry was cursing the whole outfit in a most unprofessional way by this time, and although I could see that he wanted to give this game away I wasn't going to let him chuck it in unless he conceded the game. After all, he was the professional and this was only my second game. I needed the practice.

Jerry wasn't handling the showery weather as easy as I was and with fairly obvious ill-grace on his part we played on in the rain. There was no one else left out on the course by this time, which suited me just fine. I don't like it when there's too many other people around.

By the time we were ready to tee off for the sixteenth hole our relationship was undergoing a drastic revision on Jerry's side. He was getting more and more rattled. In fact it was becoming loud and clear that this was to be our last game together for a while, regardless of what the score was. The spirit was going out of the game. My golf shoes were getting a bit uncomfortable by this time, too, and I had to take one of them off and carry it in my bag between greens (short-grass areas around flags!).

And then, guess what! — I made a terrific shot with my six-iron, right up onto the seventeenth green. Right up by the flag!

Ended up seven shots to his nine because he loused up all his putting and his ball kept rolling round the edge of the hole without going in. I'd beaten a professional golfer on a par-five (whatever that was) hole on my second game of golf. No one was going to believe me! I was as pleased as a hungry dog with a skinned possum!

Jerry was not so pleased. In fact it was there on the seventeenth green that we fell out with each other for the time being. Jerry gave up blaming his putter and the weather and the sand-traps, and started blaming me. Told me I ought to go back to my pig-hunting because I had the appropriate manners for that.

I pointed out that I had as much right to play golf as the next man. And he said I'd never play a decent game of golf if I lived to be a thousand because it required at least *some* idea of how to conduct yourself, and besides I'd be lucky to ever find anyone silly enough to want to play golf with me.

And he was standing right there! Getting his temper in a tangle over losing one hole of golf out of eighteen! Fair go! Makes a bloke begin to wonder if Jerry might not be in the wrong sort of occupation for someone with his temperament.

I'd got used to having to wait for him to finish letting off steam so we could start on the next hole. It had become part of the game. I went to put the flag I was still holding back in the hole. I wasn't listening to him any more but I thought I heard him say something that sounded like "little squirt".

"What did you say just then?" I asked, going over to him.

"I said you've been nothing but a bloody nuisance every minute you've been on this golf course!" he shouted. "And I also said you needn't bother coming back again, embarrassing everyone with your crappy clothes and junky clubs, you pesky little squirt. That's what I said! Because if you do, I'll throw you and your ridiculous clubs out the gate a bloody sight quicker than . . ."

That's as far as he got, because I interrupted him.

I don't happen to like people who make nasty remarks about the way other people are built, and when they do that to me I get an irresistible urge to give them a taste of what it's like to be on the receiving end of it. And before I could decide whether or not to do it, I found myself explaining to this tantrum-throwing, bony-legged, herring-gutted, mingy-muscled, dry-jointed, dangle-armed, frilly-handed, partial-plated, pinch-nosed, narrow-eyed, thick-skinned, nail-headed, short-winded quitter that I strongly objected to being called a pesky little squirt by a sour-natured, shallow-minded, toy-smashing, nasty-tongued, over-protected mummy's boy. "And if you want a real lesson in personal-remark-making," I added, "Just start me off again and I'll give you a read-out on your own praise-seeking, breast-hungry, toilet-haunted personality that'll take your petulant little mind off other people's short-comings for a while. But I advise you to get on with the game and forget the insult-slinging, at least until you grow up a bit."

Jerry had been making a couple of threatening advances towards me, and pretended not to be listening half the time, but I knew he wouldn't do anything when it got right down to it. I'd had him out pig-hunting and played nearly two games of golf with him. I take a bit of stopping, once I get wound up like that. I don't like it when people start making personal remarks about the way I'm built. I just don't like it.

Jerry was looking a bit sulky on it, but he didn't have any more to say for himself. We did play the eighteenth hole, sort of. I teed off, having won the last hole, and hit my last ball over the boundary fence into a creek. Jerry hit a beauty, right up near the green! Then when I asked him if he'd lend me a ball to finish the game with he just walked off up the fairway without speaking. So I hunted around in some long grass to try and find another ball, and when I looked up Jerry was halfway across to the clubhouse in the rain.

So I conceded him the game and followed.

He'd disappeared somewhere by the time I got to the clubhouse and I decided not to try and find him to thank him for the game. I threw my clubs and shoes into the ute instead, and went home to get some dry clothes on.

Poor Jerry, I felt a bit sorry for the bloke in a way. It was going to take a fair few double whiskies to settle him down after that game.

I'd found out a lot more about golf that day, but the main thing I'd learnt was that if you start getting rattled about the game, it can bring you badly undone, no matter how good you are.

Anyway I've got Arney interested in golf now, and nothing ever rattles him.

June
CHAPTER
THREE

ONE

I think I might have stumbled onto the answer to a lot of the problems golfers have been having with this game ever since it started. I won't keep you in suspense — it's all a matter of having the right gear for the job. Arney's been telling me that for years, but who'd have thought it would have applied to a thing like golf!

Sheer coincidence, the way it happened. I was over at Jimmy Wright's timber-mill a while back and somehow or other Jim found out that I was prepared to sell that row of pine trees along the road boundary after all. For a thousand bucks. They were getting too big and keeping the sun off the grass, and that. It turned out that the most Jim could afford to pay for them, in actual cash, was six hundred dollars.

I had to go into town that day to get a replacement dog chain, and the upshot of it all was that I suddenly found myself walking right past the sports shop with six hundred dollars unexpectedly in my pocket. A man'd have to be a down-right fool to turn his back on a providential thing like that!

So I went right in and bought them there and then. You don't just run into perfect sets of golf clubs to suit a bloke my size every day of the week, do you now! Picked up a trundler and half a dozen of the cheaper balls while I was in the shop, to save me having to come back later.

You can imagine what my next move was. I couldn't wait to get home with my new clubs. That is until I got there. The missus — Haven't I told you about the missus yet? Well, she's bigger than me. Five-foot-eight in her socks, she is, and hefty with it. Takes a bit of standing up to, I can tell you, especially when you're a bit on the short side like me. Glad I don't have to stand up to her very often — Well anyway, as I was saying, the missus takes one look at my new clubs and trundler and bag (forgot to tell you about the bag), and she goes quiet. And when my missus goes quiet, she goes QUIET! I just can't handle too much of her kind of quiet.

It took a bit of doing, but I finally got her talking again. Cost me, though. It cost me nine yearling heifers. Three-month holidays don't come cheap these days. She'd been hinting how nice it'd be to go and visit her sister, who was six months under way with her third baby. The missus wanted to go and stay with them and look after the family while her sister . . . you know the sort of thing. I couldn't understand her wanting to do that, any more than she could see why I like to play the odd round of golf occasionally, but I wasn't going to stand in her way. She didn't stand in mine and I appreciate that.

Three months was a long time, but it was hardly worth her going for any less. That was the only snag, her sister lives in Perth. Perth — Australia.

So the missus booked a seat on a plane to Australia, leaving in five days' time. She arranged connecting flights and stuff in Aussie, cabled them she was coming, then rang them up to make sure they'd got the cable. And then she turned her attention to organising me and the farm while she was away.

You know what they're like, these women. They get the idea

in their heads that a man'd be utterly helpless without them around to keep an eye on him. She wrote out all kinds of lists and instructions and letters to be posted while she was away and reminders and post-dated cheques and directions and dates and addresses and phone numbers . . . I lost all track of it in the finish. No, that's not right, I lost all track of it as soon as it started.

By the time she left, there was a pile of paper on the kitchen table that would have confused a computer. Whenever she reminded me about something, I remembered she'd reminded me about it already, and I'd already forgotten. She even rang up the golf club to get them to remind me to put gas in the ute on the way home because we had to leave early next morning to get to the airport in plenty of time. Aren't women beauts!

The last thing my missus said before she got on the plane was that I was to be sure and remember to pick up the list of groceries she'd tucked into my pocket before we'd left home. You'd have thought she was going away for three years, instead of three months.

By the way, while I think of it, did I tell you the missus and I have never had any kids? Well in case you're waiting for any to crop up somewhere along the line, forget it. We gave up trying in the finish, it was getting too . . . but that's got nothing to do with golf.

I stopped for a few holes of golf on my way home to clear my head of all that over-remindering.

The cows were all dried off for the winter. And at last I had my own set of clubs, exactly the right length and everything, and nothing to do but use them. When I ordered them they measured up . . . Eh?

Yes, well, did I tell you that I tried to talk Arney into in vesting in a set of the right-sized clubs for himself? He wouldn't be in it though. Reckoned the old ones I'd started off with would be plenty good enough for him. No pride, Arney.

Not that he wasn't keen on the game. Hell, we were out there at the golf course at least three mornings a week, waiting for it to get light enough to find the balls we'd hit off while we were waiting. We had to do it that way at first because, for one thing, we'd applied for membership in the club and didn't want to louse up our chances by getting caught doing anything unorthodox before it came through. And for another thing, it was the Mt. Garlon Club, where Jerry Marshall operated, and we'd decided to keep out of his way in the meantime, to save embarrassing him. (He'd actually moved on from there weeks before, but we didn't know it at the time).

So we'd park the ute out on the road behind the course, play a few of the back holes and then nick back over the fence and away before anyone even arrived at the club.

Arney was a great bloke to play golf with. He had a bit of trouble picking up the finer points of the game, but he was as keen as I was, dead easy to beat, and a good loser into the bargain. We had a lot of good games together, Arney and I.

There wasn't much competition in our golf. If one of us played a good shot, the other one was just as pleased. If one of us goofed, we both got rueful. When one of us won a game, we both felt victorious, then we consoled together over one of us having lost it. It was as though each of us played on both sides. Sometimes if Arney had a tricky one to get out of the rough, we'd decide that I'd better play it because I was better at those ones. And if there was a shot Arney liked the look of he'd say, "Here, give us a go at that one, Lance. I think I can see what it needs!" And we gave each other a fair bit of cheek and abuse and advice and argument all the time we were playing.

I always try and avoid giving myself any kind of a build-up but if I don't tell you that my game improved out of all recognition, you'd have to go and ask Arney; so I'll save you the trouble: My game improved out of all recognition! I cracked 'em up the middle of the fairways, chipped 'em up onto the greens, and putted 'em in from twenty — thirty feet! Quite a few times. And I put most of it down to the fact of my new clubs.

Arney was pulling off a few good ones, too. You had to watch him, one shot in every hundred or so of Arney's was brilliant, and we never knew when one of them was going to happen. And he was real deadly with a putter at any time!

Then some things happened that changed everything. Two good things and two bad ones.

The first good thing was that our membership of the Mt. Garlon Golf Club was approved and we became fully-fledged probationary members. We could quite openly bowl up and play golf any time we felt like it.

Our first legitimate game, when we could go right round the course in broad daylight without worrying about getting caught, was a great occasion for Arney and me. We turned up at the clubhouse, parked the ute in the car park, changed out of our gumboots into our golf shoes in the changing room, and fronted up to the first tee ready to get stuck into our best games yet.

After a short consultation about who was going to have the honour of teeing-off first, away we went. My first ball was shorter and straighter than Arney's. I think he was trying to celebrate the occasion by reaching the green in one, and he might have done it, if it hadn't been for the trees. He clouted that ball so hard it made me wonder why it didn't burst. But it wasn't straight. It sailed into the trees on the right, a hundred and fifty yards up the fairway, and then after a while it came sailing out again, into the trees on the left.

I took over that ball because I'm better at the tricky ones, and

Arney took mine because he likes them out in the open where he can get a decent swipe at them. I found his ball, right behind a tree, and fluked it out onto the fairway with one chip. Arney hit my ex-ball off the fairway with his two-wood; hit it into the trees further along.

My third shot went right up towards the green, good old six-iron! Arney yelled out that it was a beauty, forty yards from the flag. So I took over my original ball again and chipped it in to the bunker on the left of the green. And I was onto the green in five. Arney over-chipped with his six-iron, and then over-chipped back again. I yelled out to him that he was using the wrong club and, before I could stop him, he had his two-wood out again and with a textbook swing drove his ball towards the green, fifty yards away. But he topped it drastically and the ball sizzled through the grass, hit the back lip of the bunker, flew up into the air and came straight down onto the green, twelve feet from the hole and four feet closer than mine, for five.

I putted — missed. Arney putted — close. I putted — just missed. Arney putted — straight in for a seven. I took another putt — eight. And Arney was a hole up on me.

Arney's drive on the second hole was one of the greats! The second at Mt. Garlon is a three hundred and fifty-yarder, with a sharp dog-leg to the left halfway along. Arney's shot sailed up the fairway, curved around the bend and disappeared from our sight looking pretty good. I took three shots to reach there. His ball was sitting on the fairway a hundred and thirty yards from the pin, slightly to the left of the centre. The wild chipper struck again and Arney was on the edge of the green for six. I was four feet from the hole for five. And again he beat me by a putt. No doubt about Arney with a putter — if golf was all putting, Arney would have been right up there with champions!

So Arney went two holes up. We halved the third for sixteen

each, mainly, we both reckoned, because of some fussy types who interrupted our game. They called us over and asked us to "stop all this shouting out" we were doing. Distracted all the other players on the course, they reckoned. That took *our* minds off the game, and you have to be able to concentrate with golf.

After that we settled down to some serious golf. We knew the holes along the back of the course. We had to swop balls once on the fourth and I still won it by two strokes.

Arney's drive off the fifth tee sent the ball so far out onto the paddock across the road it wasn't worth going to look for, so we didn't count it. His second drive carried the ball and half a shovelful of turf about twenty yards up the fairway. Mine was only twice as far. We were over-trying, so we sat on a bank and consulted about this turn of events and watched four obviously-experienced blokes play on through. It looked to us as though they weren't hitting them as hard as we were, but their balls were going further. So when they were safely out of range, we fetched our balls and started the hole afresh.

My drive wasn't too bad at all but Arney's shot flew straight and low, and bounced right between two of the other players up the other end of the fairway. A terrific shot! Awe-inspiring! But not as far as they were concerned. They didn't even wave back to us. Anyway we decided to make it a rule that before each shot we had to remind each other not to try and hit them so hard. It worked, too, every now and again.

We'd discovered an important thing about golf: It's not how hard you hit the ball, but how well you swing the club.

It took us a little longer than it would have to finish that game, because whenever our golf seemed to be going off again, we sat down and waited for someone else to play past us, so we could watch how they did it. We picked up two different lots of free lessons that way. The first was lessons on golf, and the second was lessons on course etiquette; they don't like you holding up their game to ask advice.

We finished the eighteen holes with me a whisker ahead of Arney. He'd used a hundred and thirty-three shots and I'd used ninety-seven. But we'd picked up so much about the game on the way round that we decided to wipe that one and start again. So we went straight from the eighteenth green to the first tee.

This time I used a hundred and thirteen shots and Arney only used eighty-nine! We'd both each cracked the hundred barrier on our first day, and after that we were seldom over it. We were also well on the way towards overcoming another barrier, but it was a week or more before we were playing golf without keeping a lookout for anyone coming.

The situation on the home front had been getting a little ricketty for Arney, especially since the day his missus arrived back from town a little earlier than we'd allowed for and sprung us loading their old jersey bull onto the truck. The abattoir truck.

Under the circumstances it was hard to come up with a suitable explanation. She was pretty fond of that bull, Arney's missus. And of course she immediately blamed it on all this golf we'd been playing lately. Women are funny like that. As a matter of fact, that bull had been ready for the works two seasons ago, when Arney bought the pedigree one. He'd only hung on to the old bull till the new one settled down, and then he let him stay for sentimental reasons; but now he was over-stocked for the winter and we needed the money to cover a golfing trip we had planned.

We got the bull off to the works in the finish, but things weren't the same around Arney's place after that. It was going to take them a while to settle down again, too, by the look of it.

Still, you have to put up with these sort of things when you're a golfer. It's got its own rewards, too, and not long after that, the second good thing happened. I got my handicap — I was on a twenty-four. Arney wasn't quite ready to start putting in his cards yet, at this stage, but he was as pleased as I was.

Not long after that the second bad thing happened. Arney's missus bailed us up when we got back from golf one night and told us that if Arney didn't give up golf immediately, and get rid of his clubs to prove it, she was going to just walk out and leave him to it. She went on about how the farm was going to rack and ruin, and even brought up that business about the bull again. She tried to put it across that golf was a bad influence on us and reckoned I ought to give it up as well. I ask you!

Arney gave up without too much of a struggle. We know when we're licked. It was probably a good thing my missus was away when that happened. If she'd been there, she might have teamed up with Arney's missus (they do a bit of that), and I'd have had a very painful decision to — don't want to think about it.

I think I've been placed on the "out of bounds" list by Arney's missus. But we know when to over-rule our wives. Arney and I have a rule that whenever one of us has to make a decision that affects both families, we get together somewhere quiet and find out what each of us reckons about it, regardless of what else is going on at the time. If the women are involved, they get invited to the consultation; but they don't always take it as serious as we do. We knew his missus was worried about me dragging him back into golf, and we knew she didn't have to worry about it. He wouldn't do it and I wouldn't let him.

Wives are a bit inclined to worry about things that won't happen.

So we sat in the ute and had a consultation about this new development in our affairs. Arney was a bit hacked-off about not being able to play golf any more, but he accepted the situation. I was hacked-off about it too. We'd been having a lot of fun. I wanted to go on playing golf. Arney couldn't.

We decided in the finish that Arney should take over my pig-dogs. They hadn't been used for quite a while now, and it's no good to a dog, being tied up all the time and not used. They feel not-wanted. It was a good time to introduce the idea to his missus, too.

We set up a dummy sale, price and all, so the women wouldn't get confused about who the dogs belonged to. No money was ever intended to change hands between us, but Arney and I haggled for more than an hour over the price of those dogs. Drives a hard bargain, does Arney. We finally agreed on four hundred and forty-five dollars for the three of them, and the Suttons now own the best pig-dogs around here.

Arney was so pleased with the deal that he came and took the dogs over to his place that night and stuffed them so full of mutton he couldn't get any work out of them when he went out hunting the next day. Arney's missus was pleased about thinking she had him back under control again. The dogs came alive again, which was a relief to me. My missus is going to like the idea too, but I'll bet she doesn't believe it till she sees it with her own eyes.

It's a good thing, consultation.

I had a consultation with Arney's brother-in-law, too. He was taking over a three-hundred-acre block of land about a mile and a half further up the road in a few weeks time, and he needed somewhere to leave a bit of gear he was getting together and graze a few head of stock he'd just bought. We made a deal that suited both of us, in spite of him having a tendency to believe that consultation means he does all the talking and I do all the listening.

ULY

Things couldn't have worked out better if I'd planned it that way. The missus was away in Australia for three months. The cows were all dried off and Arney's brother-in-law was feeding-out for me in return for a bit of grazing I wasn't using anyway. A pretty good situation for a bloke with a just-broken-in set of clubs and a handicap that could use a bit of pruning. The only thing I was short of was money, and I soon took care of that.

How?

Heifers, if you must know. I decided to adjust my herd-replacement scheme. I sold off six of the heifers. That left me with only two, so I let them go as well. Didn't get quite as much for them as I would have if I'd hung onto them for a few months, but that's neither here or there.

Now that I had the financial side of things taken care of, all I had to do was play golf. And that's what I did. I played on every golf course within a hundred miles of Mt. Garlon, and picked up a lot of experience and confidence, which is very important in golf.

You meet a lot of different people in the time it takes to lower your handicap from twenty-four to eighteen. And nearly all the people I met on the golf course were good value. I discovered that most golfers have good manners.

One of the exceptions I ran across was a bloke called Don who conned me into a game at the Wairakei course one afternoon. I should have woken up to him when he put it on me for a game in the first place, because he kept saying how he wasn't much good at it, and his gear was just about worn out. But you have to learn some of these things the hard way, I suppose.

This Don had no sooner got me onto the first tee than he had me agreeing to a dollar a hole. Talked me right into it, he did. That didn't help my first drive, I can tell you. And by the time we'd gone three holes all I could do was wait for it to be all over and done with. He laughed and joked and then pretended to be bashfully astonished whenever he outplayed me, which was just about every shot. He dropped the flag onto the green just as I was making a tricky putt and then apologised so abjectly that I felt like giving him his eighteen dollars and leaving him right where he was.

I'm glad I didn't do that, though, because it turned out to be an interesting game, that one. Pure luck, it was. We were just walking up to the fourth green when the wheel came off his trundler.

You should have seen him! His good humour disappeared completely and was replaced with an exploding violent temper, and somebody called "That Bloody Frank" was never going to get the loan of *his* bloody clubs again, or his lawnmower, either, for that matter.

I won the fourth hole by a stroke. And the fifth. And the seventh. We had no way of keeping the wheel on Don's trundler and its kept coming off and tipping the whole outfit over. And every time it happened this Don got more worked up over it. His game went all to hell.

By the time we'd gone sixteen holes "That Bloody Frank"

was copping the blame for everything that had gone wrong around Don for many years, and I'd been listening to some pretty unpleasant remarks about him. At last I couldn't help putting in a word on This Bloody Frank's behalf.

"This Frank a mate of yours, is he?" I asked Don.

"He thinks he is."

"Making a bit of a mistake there, isn't he."

"He won't be making any more mistakes with my gear. He won't be getting the chance, the bludgin' bastard."

"Lucky for him, in that case."

"Him? What do you mean by that?"

"Well if he's been thinking you're a mate of his, he's been pretty wrong, hasn't he? When you tell him what you've been telling me, he'll know where he stands."

"What are you trying to get at, mate?"

"Don't call me mate, please. I've been hearing how you talk about your mates and I don't happen to like people who make rude personal remarks about other people, especially when they're not there to defend themselves, and more especially when the remarks are made to someone they don't even know, and more especially still when they're made by a back-biting, truth-twisting, word-curdling, grudge-holding, booze-bludging, ugly-tempered, faulty-reasoning. . ."

I was just getting wound up on him when he suddenly let out a bellow and took a back-handed swipe at me with his golf club, making me jump backwards out of the way. ". . . bumble-footed, sausage-legged, dandruff-shedding, watery-eyed, ear-probing, saggy-panted, armpit . . ." Another bellow and swipe with his club and jump back out of the way. ". . . sniffing, fun-smothering, game-spoiling, money-hungry. . ." Another swipe, bellow, jump. ". . . advantage-taking, work-dodging, pie-eating, bulging-bellied, . . ." This time he threw the club at me, just missed, and charged at me roaring like a bull. I dodged around a small clump of trees. He was as easy to avoid as a blind bear. "Dull-witted, flat-headed, fat-necked, melon-jawed, mottle-faced . . ." I peeked around the edge of the trees. He was picking up his club. ". . . hairy-nosed, fumble-fingered . . ." He was putting the club back in his bag. ". . . bulgy-hipped, two-tongued, . . .", he was striding off towards the clubhouse. A quitter. He was shouting some kind of watery threats at me, but they didn't work. ". . . mean-hearted, ear-bashing, brow-beating, wheezy-lunged, jelly-livered, angina-prone, varicose-veined, sour-blooded . . ."

I stood on the rise and abused him till he was out of earshot. By this time I realized that there were golfers here and there, still as chessmen, standing around the golf course watching it all. I got my clubs and snuck cautiously round to the car park and got in the ute and drove through to Rotorua for a change of scenery.

Ever since then I've been a bit more careful who I commit myself to eighteen holes of golf with. A man could have got himself injured playing golf with a bloke like him! Glad they're scarce.

Must tell you how I met Trev. I was staying in a motel near the Timberlands golf course at the time, and one morning just after daylight I was out doing something about my chipping at that raised eleventh green they've got there, and down through the mist comes this ball — Plop! — right beside me. I waited to see who it was and along comes Trev. And in less than no time at all we were old cobbers.

We hung around the course all that day, playing shots and yarning; and by the time I dropped him off at his place that afternoon, we knew I'd be calling round to pick him up every morning. Trev was just a whisker shorter than me, five-foot three and three-quarters.

We played every day, Trev and I. He hadn't been playing long and I helped with his game whenever I could. It's good to see someone's game improving because of something you've showed them. Trev wasn't what I'd call a really dedicated golfer. For instance he didn't like playing if it was raining too hard, or too windy or cold. And some days he'd want to knock off after the first eighteen holes, but I could usually find someone to go round with in the afternoon.

Trev's health wasn't the best. He worked in some kind of office job and had ended up going under with some sort of nervous disorder and chronic ulcers. They'd stuck him in a sanitorium for a while and got him straightened out a bit. Then they gave him six months leave of absence, put him on a diet and told him to take up something, like golf, for exercise.

When Trev said his health wasn't the best, he wasn't kidding. He couldn't handle too much of the nineteenth, and he couldn't eat most things. He had to stick to his diet or his insides'd play up on him something terrible. He had to take pills every few hours, and his wife and sister watched him carefully, on doctor's orders, to see that nothing was allowed to worry him. He wasn't even allowed to carry money around, in case he started to worry about it.

Before I met Trev I thought my missus worried too much, but she's kindergarten stuff compared to him. He worried about not having enough to worry about, most of the time. And every time he found something to worry about, they took it off him, so he had to find another thing to worry about. It seemed to be a constant running battle between him, and the doctor, his wife, and his sister. Trev was badly outnumbered.

But most days it wouldn't stop us doing whatever we wanted and we got to going further afield to play golf and just generally groove around together. His missus and sister didn't like the idea much. In fact they reckoned I was a bad influence on Trev, but we couldn't see any harm in it.

By the time we'd been knocking around together for a few days, it felt as though we'd never done anything else. I could just about tell what Trev's score was going to be that day as he was climbing into the ute in the morning. He was deceptive, Trev was, he was very frail-looking and there was nothing of him, but in a way he was as tough as they come. He needed to be tough, too. I never saw a bloke punish himself like he did. He had to be the very best worrier I ever saw. They gave him pills to keep him from worrying, and every time I picked him up, they gave us a little bottle of pills for the day. Fair go! Those women were a pair of beauts!

"The doctor said he has to take his pills every day at midday or he'll slip back into one of his depressions," they used to say.

The same doctor had told Trev that if he let himself go on worrying he'd find himself back where he'd started. It was a bit of a nuisance, those pills. Every morning when we left for the golf course, we had to go through the business of being given the pills and told to remember to take them at midday; and every night we had to remember to chuck them out the window before we got back to Trev's place.

I got to know Trev pretty well because we liked to do a lot of talking, and the better I knew him the more I liked him. And boy, could that bloke worry! I used to listen with amazement when he was telling me some of the things they'd done to him to try and stop him from worrying.

Telling a bloke like Trev not to worry was like telling a broken leg to go away. It was the thing he was best at, and they were doing their best to take it away from him. And whenever they succeeded, it left him wondering if he was going mad, and he'd have to find something new to worry about because that was the worst of all.

We had one good break, the doctor pronounced that it was very good for Trev to be involved in golf because it took his mind off his anxieties, and his womenfolk couldn't object when we wanted to go out any time it got too heavy for him at home, which was nearly all the time. That worried him too.

The better things got for Trev, the more he worried; and the worse they got the less he worried. Whenever something *worth* worrying about happened to him, Trev stopped worrying. In fact he was downright relieved. He *should* be worried. He was sane! And then he'd start looking happy and smiling, when he should be looking scared and nervous. This would cause people to think he was taking the micky out of them, and they'd get angrier. And Trev would get more relieved still, and they'd get angrier still, and . . .

This happened to us at the Frankton Golf Course one day when we'd called in for a quick game. There were a few other players around and we had to wait for a while before it was our turn to start.

I got us a couple of balls out of my golf bag and we both teed off with my four-wood, which Trev was getting a bit handy with. We went off up the fairway and when I'd played my second shot, I looked around to see where Trev was and there was a bloke standing there talking to him. It looked a bit strange so I went over to see what was up.

". . . don't believe that!" I heard the bloke say as I arrived there. "What sort of a yarn are you trying to spin me?"

I saw that Trev was trying not to smile with relief, and failing. I also saw that it was getting under this bloke's skin.

"I'm not trying to spin you a yarn at all," Trev smiled. "It was a genuine mistake."

"Well where the hell's yours, then?" demanded the bloke.

"They must be where I left them," grinned Trev, now so relieved he looked years younger that I'd ever seen him.

"What sort of an answer do you call that?" said the getting-angrier bloke. "Are you trying to be smart or something?"

"No," said Trev radiantly. "I tell you it was a mistake."

"I'm reporting this to the club secretary," said the bloke, and he grabbed Trev's trundler and started away with it.

I said, "What's going on?"

The bloke looked round at me. "Who pushed your button, Shorty?" he snarled. "You just keep out of it and mind your own bloody business!"

Now I don't know whether I've mentioned this before, but I don't happen to like people calling me Shorty. Only my closest mates can do that and get away with it. And this pidgeon-toed, bandy-legged, slump-chested, round-shouldered, red-necked, over-nourished, under-worked, broken-winded baboon was certainly no bloody mate of mine. And if he wanted to be told any plainer that, just try calling me Shorty again and I'd explain to the hammer-headed, twit-faced, big-nosed, cross-eyed, greasy-haired, comic-reading, superman-dreaming cowardly great standover-man exactly why he never *will* be any bloody mate of mine, either.

By the time I'd given him this short preliminary outline of what I think of people who make rude remarks about other people's height, more people had begun arriving on the scene and everybody wanted to get in on the act. Spoiled it just as I was getting warmed up.

I'd had to deliver most of these few brief remarks over one or the other of Trev's shoulders because he'd got in front of me and was trying to divert my attention. I'd assumed he was heroically attempting to stop a fight from developing, but he was only trying to tell me he'd taken this bloke's trundler by mistake, and he was merely claiming his property back. What was the bloke doing while all this was going on?

He was standing there copping it with his mouth open so he wouldn't miss anything. I'd picked him from the start. He was harmless. He thought we'd be easy to stand over because we were little blokes, that's all. You get to know those types when you're short.

In the finish they dragged us all up to the clubhouse to "thrash the matter out". All that had happened was that Trev had grabbed the wrong trundler near the first tee and he'd just discovered his mistake when the bloke saw Trev with his clubs and decided to lean on him a bit. Us little blokes get a lot of that sort of thing. Trev's trundler was sitting where he'd left it. Didn't look anything like the other bloke's either. His was blue, the other bloke's was red.

We could have stayed to play out our game, but we didn't. We decided to take a run over to Tokoroa and play there.

It wasn't the incident with the golf clubs that had got that bloke worked up into a rage, it was Trev responding to his bullying with such obvious relief that he assumed he was being laughed by a weedy little joker trying to add insult to injury.

Trev seemed to think I'd done something remarkable, but coming from him that could mean anything. Driving along in the ute Trev said, "You sure rocked that guy back there, Shorty!"

"I hope he got the message."

"I didn't know you could curse like that. I never heard anything like it! Were you really *that* angry with him?"

"Yep."

"Just for calling you Shorty?"

"Yep."

"But I call you that — what's the difference?"

"I don't know, Trev," I told him. "I just can't help it. I hear someone make a remark about the way someone's built and next thing I hear myself getting stuck into them. There's nothing I can do about it. I don't decide to do it, or anything. All I'm aware of is how bad that sort of thing is and I only want to show them what they're doing. Give them a decent dollop of it. Hope it makes them think. Maybe they won't do it next time. I don't know. It's got me into a fair bit of trouble in my time. I stay at home mostly, in case it happens. No one except my missus and my mate Arney has ever believed that I don't do it on purpose. Most people think it's because I'm super-sensitive about my height, but I'm not so sure about that. Any kind of remarks about the way anyone's built can spark me off."

"I've been being called Shorty all my life, and worse. I just take it," said Trev.

"I know, but you've never liked it, have you."

"I've just got used to it, I s'pose."

"I don't think I could ever get used to it. People have got names. Greeting anyone by naming their physical shortcomings is a great way to open up a conversation! It's the same as going up to a black-skinned bloke and saying, 'G'day Blackie!' or a person with one eye and saying, 'G'day One-eye!'"

"What about when your mates call you Shorty?" asked Trev, curious.

"It doesn't make me go mad, they're only trying to be friendly, in a funny kind of way. I wouldn't do it to them, though."

"Like if someone calls we Worrier," said Trev.

"No, that's different. It's not a physical thing you can't do anything about, it's more of an attribute. Still bloody rude, all the same. It's the difference between reminding someone what they are, and reminding someone what they're like. You can't do anything about what you are, you're stuck with it. People criticise God when they make rude remarks about the way other people are built, I guess that's what I'm trying to say."

"I couldn't change being a worrier," gloomed Trev. "I'm stuck with that."

"No you're not," I said. And I felt him go cautious in the ute beside me.

"Anyway," I told him, "there's only one person I know who I actually enjoy calling me Shorty."

"Who's that?"

"You."

"Why?"

"Because you're the only one I know who's shorter than me."

We laughed a bit and left it at that.

A couple of mornings later when I called in to pick up Trev, his missus met me at the door and said that he wouldn't be coming out with me again. He was being transferred to Christchurch, where they had a machine that would stop him from worrying.

"A machine! You're kidding!"

"No, we're waiting for the taxi to take us to the airport."

"Where's Trev?"

"I'm afraid you won't be able to see him. The doctor's with him now, giving him a sedative for the journey."

I sat in the ute and watched them bundle Trev into a taxi. I was blown away. A machine!

I sat there for a while after the taxi left. How long had I known Trev? Nine days? Couldn't believe it, seemed like at least a year.

I turned the ute round and headed for home.

I sure hope Trev finds the right thing to worry about one of these days. I was going to miss my little cobber.

I couldn't have stayed away from home much longer. I hadn't realized how much money I was getting through. The ute was costing me a lot to keep on the road. It was always in some garage or other getting something fixed up, and those blokes can charge like a wounded bull! Motels and eating out all the time — I suppose it all adds up. This lot did anyway. It added up to the fact that I'd spent more money in a month playing golf than the missus took for three months in Aussie. And that included her airfares.

Not that I'm complaining, mind you. It was worth every cent of it as far as I'm concerned. But that didn't alter the fact that nearly all the heifer-money was gone by the time I got home.

I'd played eight hundred and twenty-two holes of golf in that first month. I was keeping my cards at that time and added them up one night when I had nothing to do. I also added up the number of shots it took me to do it, but you'd only get the wrong impression if I told you how many it was.

There was a great wad of mail in the box at the gate. I added it to the pile on the kitchen table to go through later. All that paper! Fair go — trees have to grow so they can make that stuff! I'd sooner they cut the wood into timber and sent me a board or two every month. If people didn't write so many letters to each other, they wouldn't have so many to reply to. It's a vicious circle, if you ask me, and it's getting worse every year. They're not getting me into it, that's for sure.

Everything around the farm looked okay. There was a note on the door from Arney's brother-in-law saying that the odd cow had started calving and he'd started milking them. Everything was just the same.

That night I fished a few letters out of the pile on the kitchen table. One was from the missus. She'd got there all right and everyone sent their regards. The rest of the letter seemed to be reminders, so she was all right too. The next letter was a bill disguised as a letter. I put the rest back in the heap and went to bed and slept on it.

For the next few days I was busy organising one or two business deals, but not too busy to keep the Mt. Garlon golf course warmed up. I got my handicap reduced to eighteen, no trouble, and also had one or two interesting nibbles at one of my business propositions.

Things were looking up.

UGUST

You've probably twigged by now that I'm not the sort of bloke to go off half-cocked about anything. In fact I'm probably a bit the other way, if anything. But this time I've taken the bull by the horns good and proper. The missus'd never have been able to see the possibilities. In fact I don't think it would have been possible if she'd been around, she'd have worried too much. But boy, is she ever in for a surprise when she gets home! I've sold the road paddock.

It was under a separate title — the only freehold block on the property, and I didn't even have to get it surveyed. Of course I had to drop the price a bit to get the cash, but that's the way business goes these days. Well and truly worth it, I reckon. And not before time, either.

The poor old ute was literally falling to pieces around me, rust-holes like maps of Australia! All over it. Dangerous! I traded it in on a new car. One of those Jap jobs. Goes like the clappers, and smooth as grease! Cheap to run, plenty of room in the back seat for the golf gear and trundler. Ideal. The missus is going to flip over it!

And you wouldn't believe the difference it makes to drift in to the car park of a golf club in a respectable waggon, instead of having to hide a scungy old ute out of sight somewhere. I think it's improved my game a bit as well. Probably because I'm not intimidated by being ashamed of my wheels any more.

Of course we won't be able to cut hay any more. The road paddock was the only flat-enough one on the place, but I've allowed for that, too. You can always buy hay. No, the only mistake I made was not doing it sooner.

It's funny when you get a brand-new car (this one's red!); you suddenly notice how dilapidated and worn all the rest of your gear is; I found I needed a couple of decent pairs of strides, some underwear, shirts, socks, a pair of shorts for playing in the summer, long socks for that, good shoes, a proper golfing cap, dark glasses, a new pair of golf shoes and quite a bit of other essential stuff. Added up to quite a bit of money, one way and another, but it was worth it just to see the look on Arney's face when I cruised up to his place in the new car with all my smooth gear on! I'd got dressed up specially for Arney's benefit, had to let him get an eyeful of this lot!

He didn't have much to say except he hoped I could afford it. His missus didn't even come out of the house, but I noticed her getting an eyeful from behind the curtains in the kitchen window. I didn't stay long. No point in rubbing it in. Seeing as I was all dressed up for it, I decided to groove on out to the Mt. Garlon Club and give the locals a blast.

You wouldn't believe the difference my new image made around the gold clubs. I was accepted! The places I got invited to! A whole new scene was opened up to me. I started playing golf with people I'd only seen in the distance up to now. Business types and that. Of course it was more expensive living, but what the hell. You only live once, after all!

One of the parties I attended was a disappointment. In fact I nearly got into trouble with the police over it. I'd been playing a bit of golf with a bunch of blokes from Mt. Garlon way. Nob hill, they call it. These blokes all had businesses or shops in the town and plenty of time to play golf during the week. And when one of them "wangled an invitation to one of Irene's parties" for me, I was flattered.

I'd heard a bit of talk about this Irene. Her husband had some sort of paper-mill set-up and he was away most of the time. Irene wrote a column in a weekly magazine. I'd never seen it, but I gathered it was something to do with entertaining in the home, or some such. And Irene was famous around the place for her parties and her wit.

One of the blokes met me and took me out to Irene's house, a big double-storied place. Irene met us at the door, called us darling, asked another darling to get us a drink, and then circulated among the twenty or thirty people standing around drinking in the big room, asking them if they were enjoying themselves darling. I suppose it saved her having to remember their names.

It wasn't only people she called darling, either. I heard her say something about a darling little cottage someone had just bought. And a darling old vintage car someone called Neil was restoring.

It was a talking party, where you help yourself to drinks from a big table at one end and then go for a walk, talking to one person for a while and then changing partners. The tricky part is that you have to think of something to say to each new partner. Some of them play it in pairs or groups. I gathered from some of the things that were being talked to me, that the ones who were best at this game were considered the most socially desirable. I wasn't going to do very well at this game. They didn't seem to want to talk about golf.

There was plenty of booze around and some food you could

help yourself to on a table at one side of the room. I was working my way towards the food table when I heard Irene say "What happened to that quaint little codger who came with Clive?"

"Do you mean me?" I heard myself ask, moving around from beside her.

"Oh, hello darling. How are you enjoying the party?" She was trying to cover up.

"Am I the quaint little codger you were asking about?" I repeated.

"Well — no, I was thinking of someone else darling."

"I came with Clive," I pointed out.

"I must have made a mistake, " she said, suddenly impatient. "Let's just drop it, shall we. Alan do be a darling and put another bottle of claret up for us."

I moved in front of her again. "I think you made a rude personal remark about me just now," I stated, "and now you're trying to avoid having to admit it."

"Well really! I think we've heard quite enough about it, don't you? Let's just enjoy ourselves, shall we?"

The people around us were starting to go quiet.

"You've just made an insulting remark about me, and now you're telling me to enjoy myself."

"Oh don't be so tiresome!" she said, glaring angrily at me.

"I don't happen to like people who make rude remarks about other people's stature," I informed her. "Especially when it humiliates them in front of a room full of people. And more especially when they're a stranger in your house and don't know hardly anyone there, and more especially still when it's done to raise a cheap laugh at that person's expense, and even more especially still when it's done by a woman who's supposed to be some sort of example of a hostess, but who turns out to be an insincere, rubbish-talking, mirror-loving, sickly-smelling, attention-hungry fashion-slave who proudly proclaims her own ignorance by humiliating one of her guests in a room full of strangers for the entertainment of people who can see as clearly as I can that she couldn't be trusted not to do exactly the same to any one of them behind . . ."

I was suddenly seized and lifted off my feet by two blokes who were tougher than they looked. They began to carry me out through the room of silent guests. ". . . their backs, you mask-faced, tilt-nosed, leg-shaving, word-wasting, pallid skinned, claw-nailed . . ." And down the stairs. ". . . bottle-necked, wrinkle-elbowed, prop-breasted, daylight-shunning, . . ." and out the door, " . . . weight-watching, empty-headed, humour-lacking . . ." and down the path, ". . . self-admiring, brittle-boned, dry-jointed, calcium-deficient, slow-healing . . .," and out the gate, ". . . booze-dependent, pill-taking, bathroom-hogging, hair-plucking . . ." and thrown into the road.

And don't come back again — or else, was the message.

I took the hint. I had a long walk in front of me, so I decided to start off at once. I think I'd got my point across.

Half a mile or so down the road I was accosted by two policemen in a prowl-car. They wanted to know what I was doing walking around this district at this hour of night.

I couldn't give them a satisfactory explanation, in case they checked up where I'd just come from. I didn't want to rely on *that* crowd to explain the situation for me.

"I've — er — I've just been visiting a lady in a house along there," I told them. "I'd rather not — er — give you any more details than that . . ."

The two policemen grinned knowingly at each other, winked at me, snidely, congratulated me on my gentlemanly discretion, and drove me down to the golf club to pick up my car.

I was naturally a bit apprehensive about what people's attitude was going to be towards me after that, but I'd never have guessed. To some I was the bloke who broke up one of Irene's parties. To others I'd given her a roasting she richly deserved and had been asking for for years. To others I'd gone there drunk and had to be thrown out . . . It went on. None of it was either accurate or enjoyable, but it seemed that it wasn't unacceptable in these circles, to be like they said I was. Funny bunch.

I was going to have to watch out who I hung around with. Most of the people I was meeting were well-enough mannered to be safe. But all the same . . .

I decided to stick to the golf clubs, where I could spot potential trouble and avoid it. I felt safe enough there.

I'd been impatient to get away on a trip up north and play some of the clubs there — Waitangi, and places like that — but what with one thing and another and all the new friends I was making I just didn't get around to it, which turned out to be the best thing that could have happened.

Two good things and two slightly-awkward ones overtook me as a direct result of me staying around what I'd fondly come to think of as my 'Central North Island Circuit!' I'd leave home (I was hardly ever there these days!) swoop down to Napier — across to Taupo and Wairakei — up to Rotorua — over to Tokoroa — up to Hamilton — on up to Auckland (sometimes) — back down through Te Aroha — Te Puke — Tauranga, and then back home again.

The first good thing that happened was that among my new circle of friends it was quite common practice to book a session with a pro when you wanted to straighten out the kinks in your game. A thing I wouldn't have even thought of, previously. I was anxious to get more distance into my drives, so I booked a session with a pro through one of the Auckland clubs.

Then the first slightly-awkward thing happened. The pro I kept the appointment with turned out to be none other than my old mate Jerry Marshall! Talk about embarrassment when we saw each other!

We went through with it, you have to in those sort of places; but for all the use it was to either of us at first, we might as well have been back there on the seventeenth green at the Mt. Garlon Club, standing in the rain abusing one another. But the vibes warmed up after we'd both been wanting them to for a while, and we ended up quite friendly.

Jerry reckoned that my wrist-timing needed altering slightly, but I found it hard to follow his suggestions. I couldn't help thinking about how I'd beaten him on a par-five hole on my second game. No matter how hard I tried, the thought wouldn't leave my head. And on Jerry's part, he was being so careful not to say anything wrong that he was getting his sentences back-to-front. We talked about golf for most of the hour. He really knew his golf, I discovered, now that I knew what he was talking about.

We were on quite good terms when I paid him and left, though I was plagued with the mischievous impulse to invite him for a quick eighteen holes.

The second good thing that happened was that as soon as I was away from Jerry I found I could try out all the remedies he'd suggested, and my game improved immediately. I got another twenty yards into some of my drives. And what's more, within a week I was playing to a twelve handicap! But it went back up to sixteen again a week after that. That's how it goes with golf.

About ten days after the appointment with Jerry the second slightly-embarrassing thing happened. No point in mentioning the name of the club where it happened, but the slightly embarrassing thing itself was simply that I got caught sneaking a bar-stool out of the clubhouse. Nothing very serious in itself, I'd have thought, but three heavy characters bailed me up and demanded to know if there was any reason why they shouldn't call the police and have charges of attempted theft brought against me.

They didn't seem to want to believe me. I told them the truth but they still kept asking for the *real* truth. So I patiently explained to them again:

"The golf pro at the Mansion Club, Jerry Marshall, who also happens to be a personal mate of mine, told me the other day that when you take your stance for a golf shot, your legs should be slightly bent at the knees, just as though you were sitting on a bar-stool. You can ring him up and ask him if you like. I'm waiting for some mates of mine and I just borrowed this stool here to try it out with."

"Pull the other one, sport," said one of these characters, "If a short-arse like you sat on that stool, your feet wouldn't even reach the ground!"

I hadn't thought of that, I admit, but that was no reason for them to start getting insulting about it. If they wanted to deal in insults, I had a few of my own they were welcome to. I wasn't going to stand there and let this hulking great toad-faced, beady-eyed, sadistic-minded, mouldy-smelling, pock-chinned, bath-avoiding, music-hating, fungus-footed, trouble-hunting, blubber-gutted, sweaty-necked understudy to a maggot call me a short-arse and get away with it. "And the same goes for your ferret-faced, shifty-eyed, fool-following, creepy-vibed, lumpy-knuckled, crack-nailed, hand-wringing, night-prowling, cheaply-dressed mate as well."

I was just about to start on the third one when he scampered off to call the police to have me removed from the club for causing a disturbance. They were out of their depth at insult slinging and had to call in reinforcements. All belly and no guts, those types.

I removed myself, thank you.

Fair puts a bloke off, a thing like that. I was miles down the road before I suddenly remembered I was supposed to meet three blokes who were driving forty miles to meet me there for a game. Not much I could do about it now, though. I certainly wasn't going back there again. Ever.

No need for me to explain why I'd avoided getting myself involved in club-competition matches. I like to be able to have a look at someone before I get myself committed to a game of golf with them, or anything else, for that matter. And I was shanghaied into my first competition match completely against my will.

I'd played a foursome with three blokes whose mate hadn't turned up. It was on the Mt. Garlon course and I knew the tricks of it, plus I pulled off a few shots that impressed me even more than the others. Won twelve holes, as a matter of fact. And owing to the fact that it's hard for a little bloke, flushed with success and free drinks, to resist when three big, friendly, well-mannered blokes assume that he's not entered into the inter-club tournament next day with their visiting Auckland club because he's forgotten to put his name forward. Especially when he hasn't got a suitable escape-yarn handy. They immediately dug up our handicapper and saw to it that the situation was rectified for me.

So there I was. Committed. My name the blackest and newest up there on the board. Wrong!

SHORTY BUTLER Local Member. Hcp-16.

You know how I feel about people calling me Shorty. But what was I going to do about it? On the way home I put a curse on the clubhouse. It might burn down in the night, with a bit of luck!

I had no time to even shave next morning. It was dog-dosing day and Arney had to go away to a stock sale. By the time I'd taken the pig-dogs down to the dosing-strip and arranged for Arney's brother-in-law to take them back to his place, I just had time to make it out to the club for the draw.

I'd actually been tossing up whether to front there or not, but there'd be more talk about *Shorty* Butler if I didn't arrive, and the sight of my six-iron sticking out of the bag a bit further than the others made my mind up for me. So I joined the crowd.

My curse hadn't worked. The clubhouse was still there. So was my name. My wrong name. I'd drawn someone called Col. Robt. Wuthers for the first game and we were fifth off the first tee.

I didn't like the look of it. Foreboding, somehow. But I was mercifully ignorant of what that name actually forebode. There was quite a crowd of players standing around and suddenly I realized I was standing right next to the strangest-looking bloke.

It was his clothes that got me first. He was wearing a pair of those strides you only ever see in cartoons, with the pant-legs tucked up under his knees into long stockings. His jacket was real fancy, dark green, with pockets and belts and pleats and splits somehow tailored into it. His golf shoes were highly polished, two-tone, white and brown, with big fringed tongues flapping over the front. He had a green spotted cravat thing arranged round his neck, and a green plastic eyeshade so low over his eyes that he had to tip his head right back to look up at the notice board. He was tall and erect-looking, and he smelt of after-shave and one or two other things I didn't recognize. I'd never seen anything quite like him.

And then the same bloke gave me another surprise. He was the Col. Robt. Wuthers I was playing against in the first game! And when we introduced ourselves he surprised me *again*. I've heard of firm handshakes, but this bloke was ridiculous; he could have held a boar between his finger and thumb! He re-surprised me when he spoke! Talk about cultured accents! The rains in Spain sounded like a mudslide, compared to him.

His name wasn't Colin, he informed me, it was Colonel, though his golfing acquaintances usually called him Robert, as he preferred an atmosphere of informality out on the links.

I told him not to worry about it, mate, because I'm a pretty informal sort of a bloke myself.

I didn't like the look he gave me when I said that, but his next surprise took my mind right off it. You should have seen his clubs! A huge white vinyl bag, with pockets and tee bandoliers arranged all over it and a big coloured umbrella holstered down one side. A forest of clubs was sticking out the top with — get this! — little knitted blue bonnets over the head of each club with the number stitched onto each one. His putter had a green pom-pom on its hat! The whole outfit was mounted on a wide chromium trundler flashing specklessly in the sunlight, and big snow-white tyres mounted on mag-type wheels.

I couldn't figure out why no one else was looking staggered at the sight of it all. Must be something you see around golfing circles occasionally that I'd missed running into so far! And I had to play eighteen holes of golf, my very first club competition match, with this lot!

I was going to have to watch this Colonel. He was strange company to me. And right off I caught him sneak a contemptuous look at my trundler and clubs. He wouldn't have wanted me to see that. You've got to be real quick to outflick a little bloke with your eyes. I had the Colonel beaten when it came to that; but as far as any other kind of looks went — I wasn't even in it.

I tried to open up a bit of conversation, but the Colonel only replied once, and that was with a short look at me. He didn't even stop whistling faintly to himself as he did it. So while we were waiting to take our turn at the first tee I entertained myself by imagining all the short soldiers who must have outflicked the Colonel without him knowing it. (A man has to do *something* to maintain his equilibrium in situations like that!) It was going to be one of those games.

Ignore that last bit, it wasn't one of those games at all. It was out on its own. Unique.

The Colonel had won the toss at birth and settled the matter of who was going to tee off first by going first. The reason for this, I assured myself, was to demonstrate to the group of waiting players that he was actually playing on his own, and I was there only to make up the legal number of bipeds.

He produced a single glove from somewhere around the Great Bag and worked it onto his hand as though he was touch typing on a slightly-unclean machine. He then drew a long glinting wood out of the Great Bag like unsheathing a sword and removed its bonnet, which he placed carefully on the Great Bag. A brand-new Dunlop 65 appeared with a dextrous flourish like a magician I remembered seeing as a child, a blue tee was selected from a magazine of them on the Great Bag. He stood squinting down the fairway as though it was a badly-cleaned gun-barrel for a few moments and then positioned his ball right at one end of the tee, away from where everyone else hits off.

Something about the way he gripped the club and waved it around to get the feel of it warned me that I wasn't going to enjoy my first competition game very much. And the warning became an alarm as he positioned himself for the drive. He was too rigidly-drilled to make any mistakes. Feet — knees, slight bent — grip, firm but not too tight — shoulders square —

elbows — eyes — head . . . You could see it running through his head like a countdown.

And before I could think of anything reassuring there was a vicious, brittle crack! and he'd produced a freshly-laundered and ironed, spotlessly-white cloth and was wiping the head of the two-wood with it while his spotlessly-white ball was still bounding up the middle of the fairway, already within easy reach of the green.

The Colonel didn't deign to sneer at my first drive; it wasn't worth *me* sneering at it. He finished the first with a birdie and was waiting on the second tee while I finished putting. I — er — I didn't do quite as well as him. Not so well on the second, either.

And so it went. The Colonel marching triumphantly from tee to green, victory to victory, drive, iron, chip and putt. Whistling through slightly-parted lips and absolutely confident of ultimate victory. He made the game seem like a mere formality. While I fumbled my way through it, muffing easy shots, forgetting the basics, half-running to keep up, like a child tagging along with an adult in a hurry.

I was keeping a sharp eye on him, watching for some kind of flaw in his game, his character — anything, but apart from over-doing the ignoring-me bit, all I'd seen so far were a couple of grins he didn't know I'd spotted. Small consolation. I was losing heart; a man can only take so much. And then something real interesting happened.

The Colonel's drive off the eighth tee caught a bad bounce and went just into the rough. Nothing too bad, easily playable, but it seemed to annoy him. Stopped his whistling.

My drive was shorter and straighter than his and I was waiting at my ball watching the Colonel walk up to where his was, when I noticed something a bit strange. When he stopped at his ball, he hesitated just a whisker longer than I expected.

Then he adjusted the position of the Great Bag just a fraction too carefully. And it was perfectly situated between me and where I reckoned his ball was.

He took out a club and, as he removed its bonnet, he glanced casually across to see what I was doing, when a straightout look would have been okay. I was far too quick for him. All he saw was me examining the shaft of my six-iron. Then he reached into the long grass with his club and chopped his ball out on to the edge of the fairway. I saw it hit the wheel of his trundler and bounce away a few inches.

Well! Well! Well! And well! Well! Well! again. And once more, well! well! well! So the Colonel was a cheat, eh! You could imagine a man being tempted to do something like that if he was as far behind in the game as I was, but there was no excuse for him to deliberately cheat when he had me utterly beaten and his ball was quite playable from where it was anyway. If the good Colonel didn't put that shot on his card, I was going to front him about it.

He was a bit shifty about keeping an eye on me while he played his next shot — his third! — but no show, mate. He didn't even know there was anything going on in the shifty looks department.

He was whistling again as we putted out on the eighth green. He wrote up our cards. I had a four, and put his down as five.

"First time I've won this hole for a while," I mentioned.

"You mean halved it," he corrected me. "No, I mean won it," I corrected him. "I only took four." "That's right. So did I. We halved it."

He didn't realize it but he'd dropped the not-speaking-to-me act without noticing. Something else on his mind?

"I don't think you're counting your second shot from the rough out onto the fairway, mate," I said.

"You're mistaken!" he snapped.

Wrong thing to say! His whole act was slipping. Even the accent.

"You're cheating," I snapped back at him. "I saw you snick that ball out of the rough onto the fairway. And I saw you try and make sure I didn't see it."

"You're a bloody little liar!" he shouted, and then looked up to see if anyone else was near enough to have heard him.

"Come on, mate," I said. "I tell you I saw you do it. You know you cheated and I know you cheated. You're a bloody cheat!"

"If you call me a cheat one more time," he grated, "I'll tear your grubby little ears off and stuff them down your scrawny little throat! If you can't take a beating without fabricating stories like that, you should keep right off the golf course. Now, are we going to finish this game or not? If it'll make you any happier, you can have the bloody hole. I don't need to cheat to take a hole off a runt like you!"

And he stalked off to the ninth tee, leaving me to follow or not. But he wasn't whistling any more. A different Colonel had fronted! He was full of surprises, this bloke. But I had to admit he had a point, when I thought about it. It was his word against mine, and if I turned up back at the clubhouse with a score like that on my card and told them I'd caught him cheating, and he turned up with a score like his and told them I was inventing it . . .

It wasn't my way of doing things, anyway, reporting someone's shortcomings to others. I followed the Colonel over to the ninth tee. I drove off first.

As I think I may have mentioned somewhere, I get a bit towey with people who make remarks about my size. I had no idea what I was going to do about it at this stage; but if I saw the chance you could bet a box of brand-new balls, I wasn't going to let it pass.

I'm not into the fierce-competition trip, but this time it was on. I was determined to beat the Colonel to just one more hole. I wanted to prove to him that a runt like me didn't need to fabricate stories to take a hole off a germ-fearing phoney like him. The "bloody little liar" and the "grubby little ears" and the "scrawny little throat" remarks weren't forgotten, either. And as we played on round the course, I composed a brief read-out on the Colonel's physical, mental, emotional and gastric state he wouldn't forget in a hurry. That was for when we added up the scores on the eighteenth. It was war. And I knew every divot on the course.

But war was the Colonel's caper, and he went on winning. Hole after hole. He parred the ninth, I was one over.

I parred the tenth, he was one under.

We halved the eleventh, not good enough.

He birdied the twelfth, I was two over.

He beat me on the thirteenth by two strokes.

The fourteenth by one stroke.

One stroke on the fifteenth.

Halved the sixteenth, nearly got him there!

He beat me on the seventeenth by one stroke.

By this time I was fourteen holes down with one to play. It was reasonable to presume that the outcome of the game was a foregone conclusion. But the Colonel had another little surprise in store for me.

The Colonel chipped onto the edge of the green in three at the eighteenth, and not a word had passed between us since our little exchange at the eighth green. Out loud, that is. I was onto the green for five. The Colonel putted to within four feet of the hole, a little carelessly for him, I thought. He lifted his ball. I putted up to the hole and tapped in for a seven. I waited for him to make his putt, but he was putting his putter in the great Bag and replacing its blue hat with the green pom-pom.

"Hey," I said, "You haven't played your putt!"

"No," he said. "I'm not going to."

"But you're three strokes up on me. You can win this hole."

"Yes, I know," he said. "If I make that putt, I win the game; and I'm not going to make it."

"You're kidding! Why?"

"I did take that extra shot on the eighth," he said, looking right at me for the first time. "And I lied about it. I apologize for that. And I'm sorry I was rude to you about it. I can't offer you any reasons for doing it because I couldn't expect you to understand them. Of course I concede the game."

And he turned and set off for the clubhouse.

Another Colonel Wuthers? I had to almost break into a run to catch up to him.

"If it makes any difference to you, mate," I told him. "I don't know why you did it, but I don't think you were trying to cheat me out of anything. And I reckon you've been pretty decent about trying to square off for it."

A nod was all he said.

And as we arrived at the clubhouse, I told him I wasn't going to mention the matter to anyone. He nodded again.

When we arrived at the clubhouse the Colonel marched straight up to the scorekeeper's table.

"I wish to concede our game to Mr Butler," he said. "I default by reason of not having completed the full round of the course."

He'd remembered my name from the notice board this morning!

Then he turned to me and said, "Thank you for your indulgence," or something like that, crushed every knuckle in my hand out of joint, and marched off in the direction of the changing-rooms. I felt honoured! Yet *another* Colonel Wuthers had appeared. How many of this bloke were there?

I saw the Colonel, freshly laundered and fully restored to his original self, waiting to tee off with one of the blokes from our club that afternoon. Poor Bernie was already looking a bit nervous, and the Colonel was whistling through his teeth and laying it on as thick as ever. I saw later that the Colonel won every hole of the game. I had a round with a tough accountant from Birkenhead and just snipped him on the last putt, but the greens were a lot closer to the tees than they were when I'd played Col. Robt. Wuthers that morning.

Whenever I find myself among a bunch of golfers swopping incredible experiences at the nineteenth, I think about the Colonel and how I won my first competition match from fourteen holes down and one to play. And I keep it to myself. Not because they wouldn't believe me, I'm not certain about my theory that he only played that extra shot because he didn't want to walk in the long wet grass with his spotless golf shoes, but it's the only one I can think of.

Besides that, I might run into the Colonel again one day, and I'd rather beat him fair and square for just one hole, than mention one of his misdemeanours to strangers in a bar.

It was time for me to take my northern holiday. It was true that I now had better friends and better equipment, a better car and a better image, but a man has to be realistic about these things. I was actually playing less golf! And when I checked up on my reserves, I found that I'd gone through a staggering amount of money just recently. In fact I was just about swept for cash. There was just under three thousand dollars incidental expenses. I couldn't figure out where it went. Must have been staying in all those motels around the clubs, and things like that.

Golf's one of those games where it can cost you more *not* to play it, than *to* play it. You can go through a terrific amount of money in the clubhouse. The meals are pretty steep, but the prices in the bars can be a real shock if you aren't used to them. Hardly any of my crowd drank beer, mainly spirits. And that stuff's not cheap!

In fact by the time I'd had enough of hanging around waiting for the occasional game and decided to take off on my northern holiday regardless, I found that I didn't have anywhere near enough money left for the trip.

A man owes himself a bit of a splurge now and again, but I had to keep reminding myself that the missus wasn't around just now, so I didn't need to feel guilty about it. I made up my mind to watch my spending more carefully from now on.

EPTEMBER

The missus was due home in about four weeks, I figured, and it wasn't like her not to have started reminding me about it by this time. I opened up some of the mail piled up on the kitchen table to see if she'd mentioned when she'd be back in any of the letters I hadn't opened yet. And it's just as well I did that, because I found out that I'd forgotten all about the mortgage repayments on the farm and the house.

According to the letter I found they'd been getting quite threatening about it because of not being able to get a reply to any of their letters or telephone calls. The missus usually takes care of all that sort of thing, but I couldn't remember her saying anything about them ever getting final about it.

They bring a lot of this sort of trouble on themselves, these business types. They send out so many letters that you can never tell which ones you should open. It's like someone who talks too much, you give up listening after a while, and then they get upset when you've missed something you ought to know about.

I rang up the finance company and explained the situation, and after a lot of superfluous talking, the bloke said they'd hold up some closure thing they had going, but I had to get the money to him within seven days. I had a go at telling him about the confusion all the mail he was sending out was causing, but he only wanted to hear about money really, and I gave up trying to help him in the finish.

They were doing me a favour, as it turned out, because they'd given me just the nudge I needed to make a move I'd been working towards for quite a while. I had a consultation with Arney's brother-in-law. I was ready to sell him the whole dairy herd, and he could have the bulls as a gift to help him get started on his new place. They were his right away, he'd been calving and milking them for two months already and he was blown away with the proposition. I told him about needing the money as soon as I could get it and he shot into town right then to see what he could do for me. Nice bloke, Arney's brother-in law. And he raised a loan from the same finance company that was hassling me for the mortgage repayments.

I thought this was a bit of luck at first. I rang the finance company bloke and told him to deduct what I owed him and send the rest of Arney's brother-in-law's loan money straight to me, or I could drop in and pick it up if he liked.

But it was too simple for him to grasp. It was a different department. It interfered with their system. He wasn't authorized. The general manager wouldn't stand for it. He needed signatures . . .

In the end I had to drive all the way into town and fill in forms and sign papers and answer a lot of questions that didn't have anything to do with it, as far as I could see. And he was trying to make it look as if *I* was wasting *his* time!

"Is that all I have to do?" I asked him at last.

"Yes," he said, "That's all we'll need from you."

"Where's the money, then?" I asked him.

"What money?" he said.

Fair go! He'd been hassling me for days — weeks, if you take all those letters into consideration — and I'd gone along with him and done everything he wanted, and when it's all over he asks me what money! You can't win.

"The money you owe me for my dairy herd," I said.

"Mr Butler," he sighed, "you haven't understood a word of what I've been telling you, have you?"

"No," I admitted, "but I've done everything you wanted me to, haven't I?"

He beseeched the heavens for assistance with his eyes, and gathered his energies with a great effort. I did the same, but I wasn't being so obvious about it.

"Look, Mr Butler," he said with exaggerated patience, "I'll see to everything. Don' t worry about the mortgage repayments, we'll deduct them from the loan money and let you know by post when they fall due again. You'll receive our cheque in the mail as soon as Mr Watson's application is processed, in about a week. Now you just go on home and don't worry about it any more."

I know when I'm licked. I went home. (The golf club, actually.)

I hadn't realized the terrific hassles the missus had been going through all these years! Dealing with blokes like that! I was more pleased than ever that I'd taken this step, it was going to take a lot of the load off us, not having to milk ninety cows a day. We can stick a few hundred sheep on the place later on and make just as much money. I'd gone over the whole idea with Arney about a year back and it looked like a pretty sound proposition to me. And won't the missus be blown away when she gets home and finds out that there's no more cows to milk!

I had to open all the new mail and play golf to pass the time, for a few days after that, and exactly a week later the finance company's cheque for eighteen thousand, seven hundred dollars arrived.

I'd noticed that the solicitor and the bank manager were trying to get me to contact them urgently, but their idea of what's urgent and mine have never been quite the same. They usually only want money, when you get right down to it.

While I'm handling all the family business, I've made it my policy never to get a solicitor or a bank or a finance company to do any more than one thing for us. Seems to be the best way. What costs you all the money with lawyers is when you tell the new one who your last one was. Gives them a chance to open up a crossfire on you. And if you keep putting money into the same bank all the time, it only seems to confuse them. As for finance companies — keep it simple. Once you get them a bit flustered they seem to go to pieces. The missus used to use the same ones all the time and we always seemed to be keeping our heads above water by only-just and a lot of worry.

And look at us now! In only two and a half months I'd straightened out our whole scene! No cows to tie us down, mortgages paid up six months in advance. Plenty of time for golf. And eighteen thousand bucks behind us! We'd never had it so good!

The missus is going to get the surprise of her life when she gets back.

In accordance with my new business policy I opened an account with a different bank in Tauranga and put our cheque in it for safety. I asked for one of the larger cheque-books because I expected to be out of the district most of the time for a while, and it was a long way to come just for another cheque book.

There was still a fair old pile of unopened letters on the kitchen table. I opened one of them. It was from the Noxious Weeds Inspector. Another looked like one of the missus's. It was. It was just to remind me about a few things that had to be taken care of, including the mortgages.

And her sister's baby was a bit overdue and there were one or two complications. Nothing serious, but she might have to stay a week or two longer than expected and needed another couple of hundred dollars.

I wrote out a cheque for three hundred on our new account and put it in an envelope to post next time I passed the store.

With all the business out of the way I was in the mood for golf. My game would start going off if I didn't watch it. You have to keep your hand in if you want to get your handicap down to single figures. I threw clothes, cheque-book, toilet gear, cheque for the missus, into the car, made sure the golfing gear was all there, and headed off.

I remembered to post the cheque to the missus, and then I was free!

It was good to be out on the highway again, heading for more golfing adventures. There's something about golf that really gets you. And it's not just hitting golf balls around, either, that's for sure.

One of the most interesting things about golf, as any golfer will tell you, is the number and variety of people you meet, especially if you travel around a bit or get into competitions. And a thing that fascinates every golfer is how quickly you get to know someone really well during one single game, whether you're playing with them or against them.

If you're serious, or if you're casual, if you're cool or uptight, fussy or careless, innocent or guilty, egotistical or humble, vain or sloppy — whatever the distribution of your attributes happens to be; it'll show up somewhere during eighteen holes of golf, whether you want it to or not. There's nowhere to hide on a golf course, and every game, especially with someone you haven't met before, is a challenge to see if you can get around this time without coming undone.

And there's no one more guarded in their speech than experienced golfers who've just met each other before a game. To listen to us talk you'd swear we'd never played a decent shot in our lives. And any fine shot we play during a game — any hole we win or bunker we escape neatly from — it was pure luck. A fluke! And when we win a game — well, we were a bit lucky that time, and the other bloke wasn't.

All praise goes to your opponent. Any boasting a golfer indulges in is usually done in front of friends, later, and refers to other games and places, with at least one reference to how lucky he was, thrown in for insurance.

Us golfers discipline ourselves more precisely than a deep-sea diver has to. We seek the advice of experts on fractional adjustments in our technique; we practise for thousands of hours; we spend millions every year on literature, research and special equipment — all in order to try and make the way we swing a golf club more perfect. And then when we step up to play the game, we vehemently deny having any skill whatever.

This would only sound strange to someone who's never been a golfer. But there's nothing strange about it when you know how very easy it is to come unstuck during any game of golf.

Many golfers prefer to play only with their usual fellow slicers, hookers, ball-toppers, chip-bunglers, bunker-bombers and putt-missers, because they don't like to embarrass themselves in front of someone they don't know.

Most beginners go through this stage, me very much included, before they get cheeky enough to venture out into strange country and meet each other in open competition. That's what I was doing — and that was the sort of stuff that was going through my head as I drove up the highway on the first leg of my long-awaited golfing tour into the far north.

That afternoon I played the first game of my holiday with a stock-agent, a publican and a sheep-farmer, at Middlemore.

In Titirangi next day I played a round with a stocking manufacturer. In Takapuna I played with an auctioneer against a dentist and a Samoan bus-driver. And the same day I had another round with an interior decorator, against a pharmacist and a florist.

A little further north I had a hard game with a building inspector, playing against two market-gardeners. I had a second game that day with a shearer, and we played against a jockey and a topdressing-pilot.

Further north still I played against a dairy-farmer and a boat-builder, with a racing commentator. And on the same course I had a tense round with a woolclasser.

Further north, a boner from the freezing-works and I played against a priest and an airline ticket-officer. The boner and I won and went round again playing each other.

In Whangarei I paired off with a boat-builder and we played a male nurse and a probation-officer. And later I was asked to make a fourth with a retired headmaster, a fencer and a magistrate.

That's all the games I managed to fit in during that first week, but after that I settled down to a bit of serious golf. And had a ton of fun. Most days I got my thirty-six holes in, and still found plenty of time to have a good look around the far north.

One Wednesday morning I was waiting around one of the clubs for someone to turn up when three women arrived. One of them came over to me, said she was Meg, and asked me if I'd care to partner her girlfriend to make up four for a game of doubles.

Up to then I'd never given much thought to the idea of playing golf with women, but why not?

"Okay," I said. "I'm easy."

And the way she laughed should have warned me.

Anyway, off we went. Margaret and I played Denise and this Meg, who kept calling me a little sweetie and saying wasn't I cute.

Borderline stuff, that.

Well Denise was a real beginner — over the ton, still. Meg was on a thirty-six handicap, but I don't know how she ever got it. Margaret was so erratic that everyone else gave up hoping for a fourth good shot from her.

And me? I was on a twelve handicap — been playing to a ten, and I was the worst of all. I went right off my game altogether. I put it down to this Meg saying things. Things like how I was a "Mini Balasteros", "good things come in little packages" — stuff like that. It was supposed to put me at ease, but it didn't work that way.

I tell you, that shiela was living downright dangerous that day and didn't have the faintest idea just how close she came to detonating the "Little stick of dynamite" she called me on the fifteenth fairway.

By the ninth we were all about level-pegging in the fifties and sixties, and the game was a bit like one of those Arney and I used to play. A lot of laughter and ruefulness and banter and stuff. Quite friendly, really, and I never had a chance to come right because every time I relaxed enough to play a half-decent shot Meg would say, "Wow! No wonder they call him the Mighty Midget!" or some other uncomfortable thing that would keep me good and jittery until next time. And every time I joined in the chit-chat that was going on this Meg would hoot with phoney laughter and say, "Isn't he just the cutest thing you ever saw in your life!" I tell you . . .

We finished two holes up on the others, Margaret and I, by

absolute luck. By this time I was keen to get away from these women. I'd gathered that it was their fortnightly day to "play up". I didn't know exactly what that meant, and I wasn't anxious to find out, either, but I still got buffaloed into joining them for a "quickie" on the nineteenth.

I shouldn't have let it happen, I knew that, but before I could extricate myself I was cornered in the clubhouse bar, with Meg breathing garlic into my face, showering spit into my drink, and pouring highly inflammable things into my ears.

"What else do you play besides golf, Lancie?"

"Nothing, really."

"Is it true what they say about you little men?"

"Couldn't tell you, lady."

"My, my! Aren't you the silent type! I'll just bet you're a real goer, once you get your little fire lit up!"

If only she knew! Another match like that one . . .

My drink was still a quarter full, but she grabbed it off me and ordered the barman to make it a double this time.

"Here, Lancie, drink up your nice bourbon. You mustn't get behind!"

"This puts me one ahead," I pointed out.

And she went into another hooting great stream of phoney laughter. I was going to have to make a bolt for it at any moment.

And just then a bloke came hurrying into the bar, took a quick look around and came straight up to us. He tapped Meg on the arm.

That shut her up.

"What the hell do you think you're up to?" he hissed.

"What do you mean, Harry? You know this is my golf day. I told you this morning . . ."

"That's no excuse to leave the phone unabloodytended!"

"Isn't Glenise there?"

"No she's bloody not!"

"Excuse me," I said, squeezing out between them.

"Oh Harry, this is Lance. He partnered Margaret in our game."

"Hullo," said Harry without looking at me. "You'd better get back to the yard. The phone's been going mad. I've had to take Dave off his truck . . ."

The other two women and I exchanged friendly waves and looks and I left the bar, the clubhouse, the car park and the district.

That was the closest go I'd had on the whole trip, and I was a bit surprised at myself having weathered it so well. The very next day I played with a sandblaster against two more women on another golf course, and didn't have a moment's worry, except when the ladies were four holes up with five to play.

They beat us by two holes. One of them was a taxi driver and the other ran a dry-cleaning business.

I don't mind telling you that the only women's figures that interested me were those they went round a golf course in. The other kind only reminded me of the missus. I found that women play a more leisurely, less-competitive game of golf than men. It makes a pleasant change, except when you get one who is ambitious to win — she can vibe you back to your first lesson, if she puts her mind to it.

Finding people to play golf with was no trouble, and I met literally hundreds of different people from different backgrounds and different jobs, different ages, sex, types and capacities. Die-makers, architects, sailors, painters, bikies, mechanics, athletes, waterside-workers, housewives, bricklayers, instructors, teachers, on-the-dolers, businessmen, contractors, fishermen, tradesmen, possum-trappers, policemen, public servants, truck-drivers, motel-keepers, Army, Airforce, Navy . . . they all play golf.

Until it was time to mosey back in the direction of home to meet up with the missus.

CTOBER

In the five weeks since I'd left home for my northern trip I'd played sixty-three games of golf with more than two hundred different people. And for the first time since I'd started playing golf, I'd had enough of it. I was pleasantly full, thank you, which is a rare condition for a golfer to experience.

In fact one of the things I've noticed golfers to have in common is that they'll all tell you they don't play as much of it as they'd like to or should.

I don't count the "as-soon-as" type of golfer in that. You know him, he's as keen on the game as ever, but he actually played his last game several years ago and he's going to spend the rest of his life intending to get back into it "as-soon-as". — As soon as he gets a bit more time. As soon as the kids are off his hands. As soon as the business gets to the stage where it can run itself. As soon as his daughter gets her degree. As soon as he gets the chance. As soon as he gets his clubs back. As soon as it gets a bit warmer. As soon as he can afford it. As soon as a Labour Government gets back in (one of them told me!). As soon as possible. As soon as they get the road tar-sealed — Everyone who's played a bit of golf in their time still seems to like the game. I've never heard anyone say they got sick of it and chucked it in. Maybe old golfers don't retire, they simply become "as-soon-as" golfers.

An interesting thought, that, when you consider the variety of people you meet through golf. It looks as though there's no way of picking a potential golfer, and yet we all seem to end up with the same attitude towards golf.

Of course, apart from the crazy mixture of individuals you meet around golf, there's the various types that are fairly predictable, once you've played with them a few times.

There's the ones who take up golf through simply needing exercise. They're usually mostly middle-aged and medium players. Afternoons during the week, you see them mostly. They've quite often been crook in some way, and nearly all the ones I've got talking to have just moved into the district from somewhere else, and bought a house out near some beach or other.

Then you get the retired bloke who's taken it up to keep himself occupied. He turns up regularly and plays as though he's making something that has to fit properly. His car's an older model in immaculate condition, like the rest of his gear, and he can keep you looking for a lost ball longer than anyone else around. Even if it's *your* ball. You never want to underestimate these blokes, they can give you a tough game. But their second putt is one of the most painful things to watch in all golf.

Then of course there's the social type of player. Usually in his late twenties or early thirties. He drives a car with a fair bit of grunt, a straight-six motor, and clocks up plenty of mileage. You keep running into them at different courses, often in pairs. They play against another pair the same as them, and no one wants to lose. The rivalry's usually a bit fiercer than they let on and they have a lot of fun trying to put each other off their shots without actually cheating. There's some pretty sharp players among this lot and they take the game more seriously than it looks. They're good company on the nineteenth and the game doesn't end until it's been thoroughly re-lived around the bar. Then they go off somewhere to have a shower, change their clothes and beat each other's score with the ladies.

Another golfy type is the candid-mannered organisational bloke, who's decided that golf's got the right things going for it. His golfing gear is expensive and neglected from being kept in the boot of the company car, and his game is about the same as it was four years ago.

"There's more to life than making money," he'll tell you, but you usually find out that he's kidding himself.

He occasionally mentions, just casually, in passing that a friend of someone he knows has just had a mild heart attack recently. And once in every three holes, on the average, he tells you how good it is to get away from the rat-race and unwind out on the golf course, but he can't wait to get back to the clubhouse and ask if there's been any messages for him. He pretends to be relieved when there isn't, and asks for the phone to put a call through to the office.

They're a hell of a strain on the telephone system, these blokes, because every time they use a telephone they organise two more calls, and for every appointment they keep, they organise several more of them.

He keeps checking his wristwatch, even while he's talking to you, but he never knows what the time is. You can ask him two seconds after he's looked, and he has to look again before he can tell you.

This executive-type golfer will frankly admit that his game isn't up to what it should be, but don't take any notice of him. His golf is about how it ought to be. He's playing a different game entirely and golf is only one of the rules.

Makes them magnanimous losers, though, and it all adds to the richness of the whole crazy, colourful carnival we call golf.

Another sort you run into is the bloke who plays golf to try and get his weight down. They can be as much fun to play with as anyone I've met. They try hard and get their share of enjoyment out of the game. But as far as losing any weight goes I can't say I've heard of it actually working. Most of the ones I've run across have been fighting a losing battle with their appetites. Hell, you'd have to play some golf to keep ahead of the food and beer some of those blokes can put away!

And many many more that you and I will never meet. As long as you can walk, golf can get you, by the look of it.

But whatever types you meet playing golf, and whatever their reason for playing it, you can bet your handicap that they're all afflicted with the same strange madness. They'll all tell you they'd like to play more of it than they get a chance to; and no one will ever look for a cure for it.

And we'll all probably end up on the "as-soon-as" list.

I've just thought of something else — there must be a similar scene going on on ladies' day that I haven't even glimpsed yet!

That's the sort of stuff that was going on in my head as I was driving home from my golfing tour in the far north. In fact I was so busy thinking I didn't bother stopping for the night. I just kept on driving and thinking.

When I left to go north, I'd been interested in getting my handicap down to single figures. Now I wasn't so interested in it. Or, to be more accurate, I just didn't want it any more. I thought about all the single-figure blokes I'd known and played with and against. They were good golfers, no doubt about that, all of them. But keeping their game up to it made them less enjoyable to play with, somehow. They *had* to play golf.

And most of the ones I knew were into gambling on the

outcome — a dollar a hole, two dollars, a jug of beer, five dollars, a new ball . . . It was competition they were into now, not golf.

Hell, we'd had more fun, Arney and I, belting found balls around our local course in just under a hundred with that lousy old set of clubs we found in the implement-shed that time. Those really good golfers never get that much enjoyment out of golf that I've seen. They have to work too hard at it.

Then I got to thinking a bit further afield, and it wasn't very long before I was wondering where *I* fitted into all this categorizing of golfing-types I'd been doing just lately.

I'd enjoyed doing the big-time act around the clubs. And being invited to their flash homes and all that, but I didn't belong among these people. In fact I felt such a nong when I remembered some of the things I'd done and said among that crowd that I reached over into the back of the car and found my fancy golfing hat and dropped it out the window. I'd only worn it once on this trip, anyway, I realised.

So I didn't belong to the single-figure crowd, or fit into the social circles. Let's see, who else had I played golf among? Hell, I'd met a lot of people since I'd got interested in the game — let's see — it was five months, getting on for six, since I met Jerry Marshall. Is that all? Seems like a year. Still, I do everything like that. Should have seen me when I took to pig-hunting! The missus had to put up with dead pigs hanging up all over the place, just so I could prove whatever it was I was trying to prove. No wonder she went quiet a time or two, there. What a bloody clown a man is!

But golf was different somehow. And I'd enjoyed it — it's a real good game, golf. I'd met more people than I would have ever believed. Me? And you really *get* to know them playing golf. I could hardly believe it when I thought about it. I've always been a bit shy of meeting people actually. Being so short and that. And how it affects me when people make remarks. But I haven't been thinking about it much lately.

I've gone for days without thinking about it! I used to think about it all the time. Don't know why, though. It doesn't matter anyway. Been feeling pretty light on it lately . . .

Sitting there driving on into the headlights I felt my back-of-neck begin to prickle with realisation. That game with the Colonel — something had been trying to remind me about itself all the time since! The Colonel had called me a grubby, scrawny little runt . . .

Wow! I should have gone screaming mad over that! But I didn't! I remember being surprised at the time that I didn't! It didn't happen . . . And it hasn't happened ever since!

Well! Well! Well! and Well! Well! Well! again! And once more Well! Well! Well! No wonder I've been sort of hoping to see him again somewhere!

The Colonel had made a rude personal remark about me and got away with it! Good luck, Colonel, and thanks!

Not very bright really, to make a whole string of rude personal remarks just because somebody makes one of them.

I began to feel ashamed and very lonely . . .

I let it rest there for the time being and started thinking about something else. A man can only take so much at once.

Besides, this is personal stuff!

There were two letters from the missus among the great stack of mail in the box when I got home next morning, both reminding me, twice, that she was coming, when she was coming, how she was coming, and what I had to do and when I had to do it to meet her. Four days' time.

That day I took my clubs out of the back seat of the car in case of luggage and was just leaving when Arney's missus rang up to remind me. They'd had a card from the missus and thought they'd better just make sure I hadn't forgotten or anything.

I was sitting in the airport at Mangere at least half an hour before the missus's plane landed.

It didn't take her long to start reminding me about things — as soon as I saw her coming down off the plane I remembered why I married her. She was pleased to see me too. Longest we'd been apart since we met. Been married nine years, too.

She took to the new car right off. I knew she'd like it, our first waggon was a red one. She couldn't believe it at first when I told her there wasn't a cow left on the farm. When I told her a bit more about what I had in mind, about farming sheep and that, she suddenly saw what I was getting at. Nearly put us off the road, grabbing me and hugging me like that! Blasted nuisance, at times, being such a short-arse.

She didn't seem to be as pleased as I'd have thought when I broke the news that the pig-dogs weren't around any more. I told her about selling the road paddock and the eighteen thousand dollars we had in the bank, in that order, and no trouble at all. But she did go a bit quiet about a fortnight after that when she'd finally worked out exactly how much money I'd gone through while she was away. Got a bit of a shock myself. It was impressive!

But I don't mind what you, my missus, Arney, his missus, the lawyer, the finance company bloke, or anyone else thinks about the money I spent on my golfing days and I never will.

PRIL

Guess what? No, don't bother — we're right into breeding stud sheep. It's a real go! Arney's selling his dairy herd at the end of the season and they're coming in with us, putting both farms into the one block.

We've already started developing our own strain of improved cross-breeds. SUTLER — get it? There's more to it than you'd think, but the missus is keeping all the records and stuff, that's the tricky part. I spend a fair bit of time showing people around the property and explaining our set-up to them these days. You'd be surprised, the number of people interested in sheep-breeding. We get all sorts! The rest of the time I'm mostly helping Arney with the practical side of things. — By the way, did I mention that we're expecting a baby? Well we are! It's due in July some time. The missus reckons it was probably conceived the very night she arrived ba . . . Eh?

Yes, well I don't suppose it has got anything to do with golf, now you mention it.

Golf? Well I've still got my old clubs out in the shed. Noticed them just the other day, as a matter of fact. I'm going to start playing again just as soon as I get a bit of free time. I was on a twelve handicap last time I . . . What? You don't believe me?

But then you were the one who didn't believe me when I told you the missus'd be pleased about me selling off the cows, weren't you! And you were pretty damn dubious about how some of my business deals were going to turn out, and one or two other things as well! Come on now, own up to it!

You've got to be pretty quick to put one across us little blokes, you know.

Anyway I've got to go and give Arney a hand. We're flat-out just now.

It's been nice talking to you. Drop in if you're ever passing this way and I'll show you over the place.